Books By Donna Schwartze

The Trident Trilogy

Eight Years

The Only Reason

Wild Card

The Grand Slam Series

Truth or Tequila

Raine Out

The Blitzen Bay Series

The Runaway Bride of Blitzen Bay

No One Wants That - May 2022. Now available for pre-order on Amazon.

THE RUNAWAY BRIDE OF BLITZEN BAY
(The Blitzen Bay Series: Book One)

DONNA SCHWARTZE

This book is a work of fiction. Names, places, characters, organizations, events, and incidents are either products of the author's imagination or are used fictitiously. Any resemblance to actual persons, living or dead, or to businesses, companies, events, institutions, or locales is completely coincidental. Any trademarks, product names, service marks, and named features are assumed to be the property of their respective owners and are only used for references. This book is intended for adults only due to sensitive language and sexual content.

Copyright © 2021 by Donna Schwartze

All rights reserved. No part of this book or any of its contents may be reproduced, copied, modified, distributed, stored, transmitted in any form or by any means, or adapted without the prior written consent of the author and publisher.

ISBN: 9798518466890

Published by Donna Schwartze, 2021

donnaschwartzeauthor@gmail.com

❦ Created with Vellum

THE RUNAWAY BRIDE OF BLITZEN BAY

(The Blitzen Bay Series: Book One)

DONNA SCHWARTZE

For my nieces who make the world more beautiful.

"Christmas waves a magic wand over this world, and behold, everything is softer and more beautiful."
— *Norman Vincent Peale*

Chapter One

NOELLE

December 20
Los Angeles, California

"What time does your mom get in?"

Lola looks at me as she sinks deeper into Downward Dog. She's been my yoga partner for almost a year. We get to class early, so we can grab the skinny part of the room that only fits two mats. For us, it's as much a social hour as it is a yoga class. We need our privacy.

"In one hour, twelve minutes, and about eighteen seconds," I say as I transition into Child's Pose. "I guess my prayers for a national ban on flying weren't answered."

It's Thursday. I'm getting married Saturday. Mom's coming in today to be 'hands-on' with the wedding preparation. Although she planned most of it from Georgia with very little input from me, she still feels like she needs to be here early to ensure every one of her commands is carried out perfectly.

"Are you picking her up at the airport?" Lola's long braids block her face as she tries to look at me under her arm.

"Yeah. She doesn't do Uber. She's convinced the driver will kidnap her."

Lola snorts. Our yoga instructor shushes her from across the room. "Your mom gets crazier with every detail you tell me about her."

"You have no idea." I sigh and then look over to make sure our instructor didn't hear me. "I wish you were coming to the wedding. I need your calm energy there."

"Sorry, babe. Howard would kill me if I missed his parents' fiftieth anniversary party."

"But you hate his parents," I whine. "You love me."

"I do love you, but I love Howie more. You'll see when you're married. It's a lot of compromising." She reaches over and puts her hand on top of mine. "Did you call the Buddhist monk I told you about? Maybe he could add some zen to the day."

"Lo, really?" I roll my eyes at her. "Steve's family is Catholic and mine is Southern Baptist. That's enough of a clash already. If I invite a Buddhist, I think the room would self-combust."

"Maybe that would be good. Then you could elope like I've been telling you to do for months. Your parents are way too involved. It stresses me out and I'm not even going to the wedding."

"We're both only children. Our parents haven't stopped being 'way too involved' since we were born. We decided to let them go crazy for the wedding and then decompress on our honeymoon."

"Okay," she says, biting her lip. "It's just—you've established your own way of living these last four years. Don't let them come into town and blow everything up. I understand not wanting to fight with them, but you have to establish boundaries. It's your wedding and more importantly, it's your life. Let them know early what your boundaries are and then reinforce them with steel because they're going to keep trying to bust through them for the rest of your life if you don't."

"I understand," I say, nodding. "I'm not letting anyone bust up this little Mecca we've created. As soon as they leave, we're back to being Southern California hippies."

"Is that what you think you are? A hippie?" She laughs as she falls out of her pose and rolls over on her back. "You're a country club girl from Atlanta who's spent four years at UCLA—one of the most expensive public schools in the country."

"Okay, okay. I'm an aspiring hippie. I want to be like you one day."

"Really? You want to be broke?"

"I want to be happy and peaceful like you and Howie."

She smiles as she takes my hand again. "We are that. I hope you and Steve are as happy as we are. Just remember, the two of you are a team and your team comes first. Don't let anyone separate that nucleus—including your parents."

"We'll be fine once they leave and it's just us. I promise."

"All right," she says, closing her eyes. "Here's my best advice: program your phone to play soothing music once an hour. When the music starts, close your eyes and take a few deep breaths. It's how I get through weekends with my in-laws. Every time the alarm goes off, I know I'm an hour closer to freedom."

"It's worth a try." I take a cleansing breath as our instructor announces Shavasana. As he turns the lights off, I lie on my back and close my eyes. This is usually the most relaxing part of the hour, but today, my mind's racing.

As if normal wedding stress wasn't enough, it's only five days before Christmas. I begged Steve to wait until next year to get married, but he wanted to set the date for right after we graduated, and my mom agreed with him. They never agree on anything, so when it happened, I gave in and let them pick the date. I've regretted it every day since.

My mom hates Christmas. She acts like she likes it. Actually, she acts like she loves it, but no one could treat Christmas the way she does without absolutely hating it. From the time she drops the last miniature-sized Snickers into a Halloween bag to when the clock strikes midnight on New Year's Eve, Christmas is her job. And she's going to do that job better than anyone has ever done it—every year for the rest of her life—until it kills her.

My childhood Christmases were a flurry of excessive activity. We barely stopped moving for two months straight—decorating, baking, caroling, shopping, and partying. And none of it was even remotely enjoyable. The only time I remember liking any part of the holidays was when I spent the weekend before Christmas with my grandma every year.

Grandma's house was warm and quiet and at Christmas time, it smelled like vanilla and cinnamon. My cousin Kit and I would snuggle on Grandma's couch under furry blankets while we ate cookies and watched Christmas movies. Charlie Brown was first every year, the one where Linus gives that speech about the true meaning of Christmas that ends with 'and on earth peace, goodwill toward men.' I never really understood that when I was a kid, but it makes so much sense to me now. What better way is there to celebrate Christmas than with peace and compassion.

Grandma died four years ago—right before I started college. Her death was the reason I chose UCLA. Before she died, she told me that 'sometimes you have to break free of what you know to find out who you are.' I still think of that every day. Moving to California freed me up to be who I always knew deep down I was supposed to be—an easy-going, peaceful soul. I've left all the chaos I felt growing up back in Atlanta.

"Noelle." Lola shakes me. "Girl, you got deep into meditation today. Or are you just trying to delay picking up your mom? Get up. Class is over."

I leap off the mat and grab my phone out of the cubby behind me. Mom's plane lands in forty-five minutes. I meant to leave class early, so I could go home and change. No time for that now. She's going to hate that I'm wearing yoga pants, hate that my hair's sweaty, and hate that I'm running late.

So much for peace on earth. Let the chaos begin.

Chapter Two

NASH

December 20
Blitzen Bay, California

"You expecting another Ice Age, Nash? It gets cold up here, but you couldn't use this much firewood in three winters."

My neighbor Sam walks around the enormous wall of firewood I've created in the three months I've lived here. I chop the log already queued up and leave the ax in the block.

"Hey, Sam." I almost have to bend down to shake his outstretched hand. He's no more than five-foot-five. "Yeah, I'm going to have to give some of this away. I've been using it as a stress-reliever, but I might have gone a little far. Do you need any?"

"I'm set, but I'll help you haul some over to the lot off Main Street. That's where everybody puts stuff if they have extra."

"I wondered what that was. People are always dropping off and picking up random stuff. Is it all free?"

"Yeah. Leave what you have too much of; take what you need. It's kind of like a swap meet, I guess. People have been doing it for as long as I can remember. My favorite time is in the summer when people leave trays of strawberries. I've never had enough patience to grow them, but I sure like eating them."

Every week, I learn something new about this town that makes me even happier I moved here. The week I retired from the Army, my uncle invited me to stay with him in Palm Springs for a while. For weeks, I'd start from his house and drive in a different direction until the sun started to set. The time on the road almost made me forget what happened in Afghanistan.

One day I found myself in the San Bernardino Mountains. I stopped for lunch at a little town a few miles from Big Bear. The minute I drove into Blitzen Bay, I felt my blood pressure drop. I bought this house a week later.

"I've got a few more sets of blocks for you inside. C'mon in." I motion him up the hill to my house.

He follows me through the new door I installed off my back deck. It's one of about a hundred projects I have to do to get the house in decent condition. I wanted to be right on the lake. The only thing I could afford was a dilapidated one bedroom house that no other buyer would touch.

"Sorry for the mess," I say, shoving a pile of dirty clothes off the couch. I motion him toward it. "There's coffee on the counter if you want some."

I head to the small sun porch off the bedroom. I converted it into a workshop until I can build a separate one in the backyard. The lathe my grandpa left me takes up most of the room. The wood clippings and dust take up the rest. I grab the two sets of blocks I carved this week.

Sam's sitting on one of the stools at the kitchen counter sipping what I can only imagine is very thick coffee. It's been in the pot for at least three hours. He doesn't look like he minds. Honestly, I'm not sure anything bothers him. Since I moved in next door, I've never seen him without a smile on his face.

"These are as beautiful as the rest," he says as he pulls a few blocks out of the bag. "You're talented. You said your grandpa taught you how to carve?"

"Yeah. I spent summers with my grandparents out in the middle-of-nowhere Texas. He taught me to carve and a lot of other things. Who taught you how to paint?"

Sam and I have started a little business. I carve sets of toy blocks and he paints them. He's been taking them over to the Big Bear resorts to sell to the gift shops. They can't get enough of them. He's donating our profits to a hospice center. I'm guessing they took care of his wife before she died.

"I taught myself. After Holly died, I almost died myself—first of grief and then of boredom." He rakes his wrinkled hands through the mop of thinning white curls on his head. "My daughter's an artist. She started me off with some paint supplies. Then I got obsessed with it. I was painting furniture before you showed me your blocks. I like doing this better. We're a good team."

"That we are," I say, nodding. "How long ago did your wife die?"

"A couple years back. I didn't think anything could be as hard as the PTSD I had after Vietnam, but losing her was about a hundred times worse. She helped me get over the stuff I saw in the war, but I didn't have anyone to help me get over her. Not that it's possible anyway. There's no getting over that woman. She was the love of my life."

My parents got divorced when I was ten, but my grandparents had that kind of all-consuming love. I haven't even come close to finding it. Of course, I've been in the Army since I was eighteen. I haven't had much time for dating. Now, almost a decade later, I'm not sure what woman would want me.

"You seeing anyone?" Sam asks as he takes another sip of coffee.

"Naw. The only thing I'm looking for right now is a little peace."

"The right woman can deliver peace to you. That's what Holly did for me. The minute I met her, it felt like my body slammed on the brakes and finally took a deep breath. She always said her peace and my chaos combined to make the perfect energy."

"Well, I'm the peaceful one, so I guess I'm looking for the female version of chaos if I'm going to have as good a relationship as you had," I say, laughing. "Maybe I could use a little of that in my life. I promise I'll be on the lookout for her."

Sam laughs as he rinses his mug in the sink. "Hey, you should come over to Big Bear with me the next time I deliver these. All the resorts are decked out for Christmas. It's really beautiful."

"Thanks for the offer, but I'm not much in the Christmas mood this year. Maybe next year."

He's still smiling, but his eyes narrow a little bit. "I struggled after I got out of service, too. If you ever need someone to talk to—"

"Izzy and Gabi talk too much." I try to laugh. I knew I shouldn't have told them about my past, but they have a way of getting stuff out of me without me even knowing it's gone.

"Gabi's not your problem. She's a vault. Izzy, on the other hand . . ." He stands up and pats me on the shoulder. "I'll leave you in peace. Thanks for the blocks. I'll work on these today."

"I'll try to start doing more than two sets a week. Getting this shack in shape is taking a lot of my time."

"There's no rush at all. It's a nice hobby. Do as much as you want to or none at all." He heads toward the door. "Thanks for the coffee."

"Hey Sam," I say, taking a few steps in his direction.

He turns around—the grin still lighting up his face.

"Thanks for offering to talk. It's a little too new for me, but I appreciate the effort," I say, forcing a severely underused smile to my face. "And yeah, I was a Ranger. Just between us, shrapnel in my knee took me out. One of my buddies died on the same mission."

"I'm sorry to hear that, Nash. My best friend died over in 'Nam."

I nod at him. I know he understands.

"Just please don't tell Izzy any of that."

"I'm so old. I'll probably forget what you told me by the time I get back to my house."

I hear him chuckling as he disappears behind the woodpile.

Chapter Three

NOELLE

December 20
Los Angeles, California

"Hey! Hey! Security!"

As I slam my car door, I start running after a security guard cruising through the parking garage in a golf cart. The airport's impossibly crowded. It took me longer than usual to find a parking spot. My mom's plane landed three minutes ago. I'm at least a quarter-mile from the terminal. She waits to text me until the plane parks at the gate. I check my phone again. No text yet, but I know it's only minutes away.

The guard stops and turns around as I close in on him. "You okay, ma'am?"

"Not really. My mom just landed and if I'm not there to greet her when she gets to the baggage area, I'll have to hear about it for four straight days until she leaves on Sunday. Will you please give me a ride?"

He chuckles but shakes his head. "Sorry. I can't have civilians in this vehicle."

He says it like he's driving a tank. It's a freaking golf cart.

I smile and tilt my head. "That totally makes sense. It's just that my mom's already going to lecture me on what I'm wearing and how my hair looks. I'm trying to limit her ammunition a little bit."

He nods as he glances in the rearview mirror. "My mom always tells me I'm losing hair. I see her at least once a week and she says it every time like she's counted each hair and knows when one's missing." He moves the notebook in the passenger's seat and nods toward it. "Get in. At least one of us should have some peace this Christmas. What airline?"

"Delta," I say as I jump in. My entire body tenses up as my phone buzzes.

Plane at gate.

Mom texts like they charge by the word. I don't reply. She puts her phone back into her bag the moment after she texts. She never requires a response—even in face-to-face communication.

Even though the security guy's pushing the golf cart to the absolute limit, I think I could have run faster. I finally see the Delta terminal as we round a corner. He screeches to a halt, almost sending me through the windshield.

"Good luck with your mom," he says, grabbing my arm to steady me.

"Thank you so much! Seriously, you saved me." I look

over my shoulder as I run toward the doors. "And by the way, I think your hair looks amazing! Merry Christmas!"

I bob and weave through the holiday travelers until I get to the base of the escalator. I'm there about ten seconds when I see Mom descending. I don't even have to look at her face—the stiletto red leather boots paired with the impossibly skinny black pants could only belong to her. As she comes into full view, I see she's wearing a matching red leather jacket that she has buttoned way too snugly at the waist. My mom can't weigh more than a hundred and twenty pounds, but somehow she still manages to wear clothes that are too tight for her.

She sees me. I smile and wave. She does neither.

"Hi Mom," I say, reaching my arms out for a hug as she walks off the escalator. She hands me her Louis Vuitton roller bag instead.

"Noelle! What are you wearing? You look like you came from the gym. I've told you before that casual wear is meant for exercising only. It should be on your body five minutes before you leave for the gym and five minutes after you get home. Did you not have time to change after aerobics?"

"I was doing yoga, but no, I haven't been home yet. We can stop by our apartment before we go to the wedding venue so I can change."

"I told you I wanted to go to the venue immediately after I landed. You should have planned accordingly. I don't trust the wedding planner at all. What's his name? Connor? He doesn't seem to understand my vision. And when did you start doing yoga? I knew California would be no good for you the minute you told us you picked that hippie school. Why you didn't go to UGA I will never understand, but I guess you wouldn't have met Steven unless you came here. His mother and I talk all the time about how we need to get you out of California and back to the South. This state is corrupting your mind."

She's walking at least five feet ahead of me like she knows where the car's parked. I run to catch up with her, pulling her bag behind me. She's already on the phone with Connor, telling him we're on our way. I can almost feel his anxiety through the phone. We finally get to the car. I click open the locks on my doors and Mom gets in. I try twice to lift her bag into the trunk before some guy takes pity on me and lifts it in. Mom hasn't looked back once. She's still on the phone.

My phone beeps and starts playing "Have Yourself A Merry Little Christmas." It was Grandma's favorite Christmas song. I close my eyes and take a deep breath—one hour down, only about a hundred more to go.

Mom's on the phone almost the entire way to the venue. I purposely take the route that leads through Beverly Hills. Displays of wealth make Mom very happy. She sighs as we drive past Rodeo Drive. My stress level starts to go down a bit but then I turn onto Laurel Canyon. As we start climbing, Mom abruptly ends her conversation with Connor.

"Noelle! Where are you taking me?" She throws her phone into her Louis Vuitton Carryall.

"We're going to the wedding venue. It's only like a mile farther."

"Did you change the venue without telling me?" She looks at me like she thinks this is a possibility.

"Mom, no. It's the estate you and Mrs. Walker chose. It's the same place as always. It's beautiful. You've seen pictures—"

"Well, I didn't know it was at the top of a mountain. How are our guests even going to get up here?"

I squint at her for a second waiting for her to realize that they will drive up here like we just did. She's staring straight ahead.

"Here we are," I say with forced enthusiasm as I turn into the long estate driveway. On the way, I point out the large parking lots at the adjacent museum that our guests can use.

"Why are you showing me that? I would expect our guests would have a place to park their cars." She opens her door and gets out while I'm still pulling into the parking spot.

She heads toward the building where Connor's standing. I stay in the car for a second trying to figure out how I can escape. I want to run away and never look back. She's been in L.A. less than an hour and I already feel myself reverting to the girl I left behind in Georgia.

Mom walks past Connor into the house. He looks at me and motions frantically for me to get out of the car as he turns and follows her in.

When I walk through the doors, Mom's frozen in the entrance. She's looking at the stunning room before us. Connor's decorated it perfectly to accent the natural beauty of the canyons framed by the floor-to-ceiling windows. There are tall cactuses lining the steps up to the makeshift altar. Each cactus is exploding with red blooms. It's perfect. I smile and look at Mom.

She turns to Connor. "It's all wrong. I'm glad I came in early because you obviously can't follow the simplest instructions."

Chapter Four

NASH

December 20
Blitzen Bay, California

"Yeah. Yes. Momm . . . Stop."

My mom's been nagging me for two months to go to my high school friend's wedding. I wouldn't even consider it if it were back in Dallas. I moved here to get away from everyone and everything I knew. I don't miss anything about Dallas except my mom.

"Nash, the wedding's under an hour from your house. I pulled it up on the Google maps. I'll email it to you."

Mom still thinks I'm a teenager. That's the last time I spent any real time with her—back in high school when she did everything for me. Since I left for the Army, I've seen her maybe once a year.

"I'm good with the maps, Momma." I laugh to myself. "I promise I'll try to make it down there."

"I told Bitzy you were coming. They'll have a place for you at the family table. It's a very high-end wedding. He's marrying a debutante from Georgia. If you don't go, it will reflect badly on our entire family."

Mom still lives in the suburb where I grew up. Most of the families have lived there for decades. Everyone knows everyone else's business. She lives in constant fear that one of her kids will get a black mark from the neighborhood gossips.

"I will go for you. And that's the only reason. I haven't talked to Stevie since high school and that's the way I prefer to keep it, but I will go to the wedding for you."

"Thank you." Her voice drops a few octaves. "It will do you good to get out of the house. I know it's getting close to a year since your friend died. I worry about you."

My heart stops for a second like it does every time she mentions him. Mikey will have been gone one year on the day of the wedding—one year since he ran into a tripwire in Afghanistan and blew himself up. I was right behind him. I remember pulling myself over to him—my knee mangled with shrapnel—just in time to see him take his last breath.

"Nash?"

"I'm fine," I say. "I tell you that every time we talk. I'm fine."

"Hrmpf." It's the sound she makes that means, "I'm right and you're wrong, but I don't want to waste any more of my precious time arguing with your hard head."

"Are you coming back to Dallas for Christmas?"

She knows I'm not, but she thinks she can wear me down. A big family Christmas is the last thing I want right now. I need peace and quiet.

"I'm not going to make it this year. Maybe I'll come in for Mother's Day. You know that's the most important holiday of the year."

"You're right about that, but I don't want you to be alone for your first Christmas after retirement. I can come out there. Your brothers can fend for themselves."

"I appreciate it, but I told you, I don't even have a place to put you right now. My house is a disaster. Give me a year to fix it up and you can come next Christmas. We'll have to get you some snow boots though. There's already at least a foot on the ground."

"I'm not sure why you want to live in that cold, but the pictures you tweeted me are really pretty."

"Texted, Mom. I texted them to you. Tweeting is just on Twitter, remember?"

"You know I don't understand technology, but however you do it, I like when you send me pictures. I'm going to have your nieces teach me how to do pictures so I can send you some of us at Christmas. And maybe we can even do that face-to-face thing."

"FaceTime."

"Right. I think the whole thing is kind of invasive, but it would be so nice to see your face again. I miss you."

"I miss you, too." I look at the time on my phone. It's later than I thought. "Hey, I have to run into town for a bit. I need to get some more stuff for the house."

"Okay, I'm going to start shopping for my boots today. And some warm socks and a snow jacket. I saw a pretty yellow coat in L.L. Bean's catalog."

"That sounds good, Momma. Send me pictures and sizes and I'll order it all for you."

"You're a good son. You've always been my favorite, but you know that's our secret."

"I do. Just between us."

"Have so much fun at the wedding, Nash. Maybe you'll even meet a woman there—"

"Mom—"

"I know you don't want to talk about it, but you need to find someone. You're a caretaker. You always have been. You need a woman in your life to care for or at least something to care for—maybe a dog."

"Yeah, I think I might have better luck with a dog. I don't think modern women like to be taken care of that much."

"That's not at all true. They might not need to be taken care of, but there isn't a woman alive who doesn't want it."

"Hmm. I'm going to have to take your word for it. Hey, I really need to hang up before the store closes. I love you, Momma."

"I love you, too, honey."

After I hang up, I shift through the mail on my kitchen counter until I find the wedding invitation. It's at some estate in Laurel Canyon. I skim down to the bottom. *Black tie optional.* I have no idea what that means, but I know I don't have it. The dressiest clothes I have are a pair of black pants and a white button-down shirt. I don't even have a tie.

Hank, the guy who owns the inn in town, is almost my size. He's got broad shoulders at least. I grab my phone.

Hank, it's Nash Young. I have to go to a wedding Saturday.

Last-minute thing. I don't even have a suit jacket with me. You got anything you think would fit me?

He texts back immediately—like everyone in this town does.

I've got you covered. Swing by when you can. Claire says she'll wrap up a couple of the candles she makes as a present. They're soy or something. I don't know, but everyone loves them. See you soon.

I look at the invitation again to make sure I'm not missing any dressing instructions. I glance down to see who Stevie's marrying. *Noelle Ivy Clark, daughter of Dresden and Helen Clark of Alpharetta, Georgia.* She's apparently a debutante. That's the perfect match for him—rich and spoiled. I'm sure they'll live happily ever after in their enormous house in the suburbs with two entitled children and a golden retriever. For some reason that pisses me off.

I think again about how I can avoid going to the wedding, but I know I can't. I promised Mom I would go. I've never broken a promise to her in my almost twenty-seven years on earth. I'm not going to start now.

Chapter Five

NOELLE

December 20
Los Angeles, California

"Mom! We don't need any more lights on the chairs. It's starting to look like an airport runway in here."

We've only been at the wedding venue for an hour and Mom's already turned it into a circus. People are running everywhere. Connor's spray-tanned face is somehow turning pale. He's tried to talk Mom out of every order she's shot at him. He has so much to learn.

"Noelle, it's Christmas. Christmas is made for lights." Mom looks back at me briefly from where she's directing the florist to remove the cacti and replace them with a row of miniature Christmas trees she shipped in from Georgia. The trees are shockingly white with blue ornaments—only blue ornaments. It's Mom's preferred color pattern for Christmas.

"Mom," I say, grabbing her arm to get her attention.

"Steve's family is more religious than we are. I'm sure they don't want the room to look like the North Pole."

She whips around to face me, her hands on her hips. When her body stops quickly, her elbows keep moving back and forth. She looks a little like a blender.

"Our family's plenty religious, Noelle. Even if we don't have to show it by all the kneeling and bowing. You know Jesus is at the center of everything I do to celebrate the season."

"Really?" I say as she walks away. "Because Jesus was born in a dark, dirty manger. I don't think he had twinkling lights and tinsel."

"They think they're so important to this wedding. Do they know the bride's family makes all the calls?" she says to no one in particular. I follow her.

"Mom, Steve's dad is the only reason we got into this estate. They only accept two weddings a year."

"That's just because he's obscenely rich, but we're one of the richest families in Atlanta."

"We're not even one of the richest families in Alpharetta," I say under my breath. I regret it instantly. I know Mom has bionic hearing.

She whips around again. "Alpharetta is a very wealthy suburb."

"I'm not saying it's not." I can hear my dad's voice in my head telling me to let her have her way. I ignore it. "We're just not one of the richest families there."

"Your dad works very hard, Noelle! You've always been much too entitled."

I watch her walk away again and say to her back, "Mom, I

know he does. I don't care how rich we are. You're the one who's always bringing it up."

I look at my phone. I'm twenty-three minutes from my next relaxation break. I close my eyes anyway and take a deep breath. It's not working. Mom blasts through zen like a tornado flattening a Midwestern town. I slowly open my eyes. Mom's standing inches from me.

"Noelle! What is wrong with you? Open your eyes this instant! I asked you if you thought the lilies would be too fragrant for Grandma Nan. You know she always complains about the honeysuckle off our back terrace. She can wear her perfume that smells like she just stepped out of a brothel, but one whiff of my flowers and she's 'highly sensitive' to smells. I swear I don't know why your father insisted we invite her. She's too old to get on a plane anyway."

She walks away again without waiting for my answer and zeros in on the increasingly wide-eyed florist. For a second, I think about saving the florist, but honestly, she just has to deal with Mom for two more days. I've dealt with her for a lifetime. The florist can take her turn.

"Noelle!" I turn around to see Steve power-walking across the room. He's the slowest person I know. I can tell by his pace that his parents are on their way here.

He leans over to kiss me but doesn't even notice he misses my entire face. He's looking up at the winter wonderland Mom has created.

"Babe," he says without looking at me, "my parents are going to hate this. You know how religious they are. They're still mad we're not getting married in a church."

"I know, babe. I know. I told you we shouldn't get married

in December. You know how Mom abuses Christmas. Let her have her way. It will be over in forty-eight hours."

"Aww. 'It will be over in forty-eight hours.' I hope you had that printed on your cocktail napkins."

The voice coming from behind me sounds familiar. My childhood flashes before me.

"Kitten?" I say as I slowly turn around to see my cousin Kit standing a few feet from me.

I haven't seen her for two years since she left to take a job in Spain. Her long hair is now robin's egg blue, but her devilish smile hasn't changed a bit.

"What are you doing here?" I grab her and hug her as tightly as I can. "We didn't get an R.S.V.P. from you."

"Only because I didn't get an invitation. And here I thought I was your favorite cousin."

"What? Mom said she mailed it a few weeks before the others, so we could be sure it would get to you in Spain."

Kit rolls her eyes. "Elle, c'mon. You let Leni mail it? You know it never got to a mailbox if it ever existed at all. She still blames me for every bit of trouble we got into when we were growing up, even though it was all undeniably your fault."

"Not all of it—"

"Every single last part of it." She points her finger at me. "Don't fight me on this. I still have the evidence."

Steve's staring at her. "Steve, you remember my cousin Kit. She visited campus right around the time we started dating."

"Yeah. Your hair's bluer than I remember."

"And your hair's grayer than I remember," Kit says,

pointing at his temples. "You might want to start dyeing it here."

Steve forces a laugh. As tears start streaming down my cheeks, I grab Kit into another hug.

"I'm so happy you're here," I say, sniffing.

Steve rolls his eyes when he sees me crying. He walks to where Mom's overseeing the installation of a life-sized Santa behind the altar.

"What's that about?" Kit says, nodding her head toward Steve.

"He thinks it's weird that I cry when I'm happy."

"Well, I think it's weird that he doesn't." She smiles as she wipes the tears off my cheeks. "Do you remember what Grandma used to say about crying?"

"That crying is like a shower for the inside of your body and if you don't cry enough your insides get stinky."

"Yes, and you have the cleanest insides of anyone I know. I love your sensitive little soul."

Steve rushes back over to us. He points at Mom. "You have to stop her."

I look at Kit. "Is there anything you can do to stop her?"

"Yeah, but it would involve me doing jail time."

"If you truly loved me," I say, putting my arm around her, "you would go to jail for me."

"Aww, Elle." She leans her head against mine. "That's how every one of our conversations started when we were teenagers."

"Katherine!" My mom swoops down the aisle and positions her waif-like body in the small space between Kit and me. "I didn't know you were coming. I'm afraid we never received a reply from you."

"Oh, Leni. I would never miss your big day." She's called Mom by her first name since she was a toddler. It drives Mom crazy. "I'm sorry. I mean Elle's big day, of course."

"Her name is Noelle, Katherine. If you need a reminder, look on the wedding invitation."

"It's funny, I never received my invitation. I'm sure it got lost in the mail just like my reply. That darn Spanish postal service!"

Mom turns on her heels and heads back to torture the decorators.

"If I knew you were coming, I would have made you a bridesmaid," I say as I pull Kit back into a hug.

"I don't want to be part of that sorority hell. I'm way too special for that and you know it."

"Way too special."

"I'm here just for you. Anything you need." She hugs me tighter and then whispers in my ear. "Even if what you need is to get out of here and never look back."

I push her back and look into her eyes. She knows. She's always been able to read my mind.

"It's never too late, Elle. Never."

Chapter Six

NASH

December 21
Blitzen Bay, California

"Only four more days until Christmas. Do you have your shopping done?"

The DJ sounds like he definitely doesn't have his done. My truck radio only picks up one station out of L.A. They've been playing Christmas music for a month straight. It sounds like it's getting on his nerves as much as it's getting on mine.

I'm headed into town to pick up the jacket and tie from Hank. From my house, it's only about a ten-minute walk into the center of town, but tonight, I decide to drive it. The temperature has dropped at least twenty degrees from yesterday. My Texas skin hasn't adapted to the cold yet.

When my truck crests the hill that leads down to town, the sight makes me stop breathing for a second. I've probably come over this hill more than a hundred times now and I'm still not used to it. Rows of Swiss chalets sit snugly in the small valley that backs up against the mountains. White lights frame the gently sloped wooden roofs. The chalets remind me a little of the gingerbread houses my mom used to decorate every Christmas.

Most of the buildings have a store or restaurant on the street-level and an apartment where the owners live on the second floor. During the summer, the residents sit on their second-floor balconies and talk to each other across the narrow street. People who don't live on Main Street bring chairs and sit under the balconies so they can join the conversation. There's usually wine and food being passed up and down the street.

This time of year, bright red ribbons wrap the old-fashioned lamp posts on every corner. The fifty-foot Douglas fir that grows in the roundabout at the end of the street is filled with twinkling white lights and oversized red and green ornaments.

The tree sits right outside Holly House, the inn that Hank and his wife, Claire, own. I pull in a spot next to the tree and look up at the lights. If anything can get me into the Christmas spirit, it will be this town, but so far, no luck.

"You coming in, Nash?" I hear Hank's voice and look over to see him standing on the balcony of the inn. He waves. "You'll freeze out here."

I wave back and head toward the front door where Claire's standing.

"Hey, Nash." Claire smiles and hands me a cup of hot cider. "Hank said you're going to a wedding tomorrow. How exciting? Is it in L.A.?"

"Yeah. North of the city—up in the canyons. Some estate."

"Ohh, fancy. That's a rich area. Who's getting married? Is it their estate?"

"My high school buddy and I'm not sure if it's theirs or not." I take a sip of the cider and walk over to the wood fire that's blazing in the lobby. "I've kind of lost touch with him."

"Well, it was nice of him to invite you then."

"Yeah, I guess."

Hank walks down the stairs with an arm full of jackets and ties. "We used to go out a lot when we lived in the city, but I haven't worn these in years. You're welcome to any of them."

"What does it say on the invitation for the suggested dress?" Claire says, taking a few jackets from Hank. "And what pants are you wearing? Hank's pants would be too short on you."

"The only thing I have is a pair of black pants and a white button-down. The invitation says something about black tie."

"Ohh." Clair bites her lip. "Black tie or black tie optional?"

"I think it said optional. Is there a difference?"

"Yeah. Black tie means a tux, but optional means you can get away with a dark suit." She starts sorting through the jackets. "But we're just going to have to work with what we've got. What color black are the pants?"

I look at Hank for help. He shrugs.

"Uh, they're black black," I say slowly. "Are there different shades of black?"

Claire shakes her head and sighs. "Try on this black tweed. It should match any shade of black."

I take off my coat and sweater and slip the jacket over my

T-shirt. It fits across the shoulders, but I don't think I can button it. It still seems okay to me.

"It's a little short on you, but not too bad," Claire says, pulling at the hem. "Cross your arms and let me see the back. Hmm. It's a little tight, but I think you can pull it off if you don't button it. What do you think?"

"Yeah. I mean, it's a jacket, so I guess it's okay. Right, Hank?"

"You look fine to me," he says, shrugging again.

"You're both worthless to me right now." Claire shifts through the ties and pulls out a solid black silk tie. "If you wear this tie, you should be able to pass for black tie optional. What time is the wedding?"

"One o'clock."

"Oh, it's a day wedding? Whatever. You'll be fine." She turns around and heads to the back room. "Hold on for a second. I'll be back."

I look up at Hank. "I'm not much on the fashion stuff. I've worn an Army uniform for a decade. I appreciate this."

"Claire's dressed me for twenty-two years now. She never gets it wrong. You're good."

"How long have you lived up here?"

"Since we bought the inn, so about five years. We took it over from Sam when Holly got sick."

"I'm just putting together now that this inn was named for her. Is that right?"

"Yeah, her parents started it back in the forties when they moved here from Germany after the war. They were one of the founders of the town." He looks over to a picture on the wall.

"That's them with baby Holly. We kept it up. Holly was a sweet woman."

"How'd she die? I haven't asked Sam."

"Cancer. She fought it off for years, but it finally got to be too much. I know Sam misses her, but he was glad to see her out of pain, too."

I nod as Claire walks back in the room. She's carrying two boxes—one wrapped in white paper with a very large gold bow and the other wrapped in tin foil.

"This is your present for the wedding," she says, handing me the white package. "It's two of my handmade candles. I signed your name to a gift card and put it in the box before I wrapped it. And this is your dinner—leftover Chicken Parmesan."

"This is too much," I say, putting the boxes down and pulling out my wallet. "How much do I owe you?"

"I know you better put that wallet away," Hank says as he puts on his coat. "I'll help you carry this stuff out."

I stand there for a second with my wallet in my hand. I'm not sure what to say.

Claire pats me on the back. "You can buy us dinner at Izzy's next week. Just go and have a good time at the wedding. You deserve some fun. And maybe you'll meet a nice woman there—"

"Claire." Hank swats her backside.

"Honey, I'm just saying Nash deserves someone to share his life with . . ."

"Well, if he can find someone as good as you, he'll have something," he says, kissing the top of her head. "Maybe someone a little less nosy though."

Claire laughs as she picks up the boxes and hands them to me again.

I put my wallet away and hug her. "Dinner next week with at least two bottles of the most expensive wine. You saved me."

"It's a deal," Hank says as he heads out the door with the jacket and tie. I grab the boxes and follow him.

Chapter Seven

NOELLE

December 21
Los Angeles, California

"Well, it's just like a dream come true."

My mom's face glows as she pauses for a second to look meaningfully at each of the reporters. They're all gathered around her in a scrum—like she's the winning coach after a big game. Their faces are expectant—trying to get at least one intimate detail of the big day. Mom doesn't disappoint.

She leans closer to them and whispers loudly, "You know we almost had to put a moat around Noelle's room last night to keep Steven away. He's finding it hard to wait until tomorrow night!"

The reporters giggle knowingly. They've been here all day—tracking our every step. They've not only witnessed our kisses—they've almost been a part of them.

It's Friday—the official move-in day at the estate for our

closest family and friends. There are twenty rooms for special guests to stay the night before the wedding. The rooms include two suites—one for the bride and one for the groom—separated by a large courtyard.

I watch my mom entertain the press for a few more seconds and then head back to my suite to freshen up for dinner. Our rehearsal dinner has become the social event of the season. Of course, that has nothing to do with Steve and me—or my mom. The glitterati's here solely for Steve's dad.

Trip Walker is a millionaire Texas oilman turned movie producer. When he got bored with Dallas, he bought a production company in L.A. and has become the Hollywood "it" man. The entertainment media follow him around everywhere. His secretary makes sure they have a full itinerary of his activities when he's in town except for his many late-night "meetings" with various young actresses and models. Every woman who meets him falls under his spell—except me. I've never been a fan.

I lock the door to my suite behind me and lean heavily against it. The room looks like a big cloud. Everything's white. It's unsettling. I collapse down on the tufted, white chaise and try to lose myself in the pile of fluffy white pillows.

"I don't think you can hide in there—unless you put on your wedding dress—then you might blend in." I look up to see Kit's face peeking through the white voile curtains covering the open French windows.

"Kit! What are you doing?" I jump across the room to help her over the windowsill. She tucks her head and does a forward roll into the room, throwing her hands in the air like she's an Olympic gymnast who's just completed the perfect landing.

"Nailed it," she says as she reaches into her pocket to retrieve an airplane-sized bottle of vodka. She grins up at me. "Yet another reason dresses should always have pockets."

I look out the window to try to figure out how she got to the second floor. "Did you climb up that drainpipe?"

"Yeah. I barely got a grip on the window before the pipe gave way. They're going to need to fix that before the next rain."

"You breaking your neck is not what I need right now." I walk back over and plop down on my bridal throne. "Do you have any more vodka?"

She hands me two mini bottles out of her other pocket.

"You know if Mom catches you in here, she'll kill you with her own bare hands," I say as I pop one of the bottles open and drain it.

"Have you seen what Leni's wearing? I'm surprised she can move at all, much less run. There's no way she could catch me."

"She looks like a toothpick in shrink-wrap." We both bust out laughing and then slam our hands over our mouths immediately. Too late.

"Noelle!" My mom shrieks from outside the door. She's been following me everywhere today. I think she senses I'm losing my focus. "Is someone in there with you? If it's Steven, I will hogtie and whip him myself!"

"No one's in here, Mom. It's just me. I was practicing a breathing technique my yogi taught me." I throw my lipstick at Kit who continues to muffle her laugh as she rolls behind the bar cart to take cover.

The doorknob rattles loudly. "Noelle! Unlock this door!"

"Go downstairs to dinner, Mom. I'll be down after I finish my yoga."

"California has absolutely ruined you!" She slaps the door to emphasize her point. "You have ten minutes to get downstairs."

Kit pops her head out from around the cart, but waits until we hear the brisk clicking of Mom's stilettos fade before she scowls and says, "Am I the only one who thinks she sounded a little too excited to 'hogtie and whip' Steve?"

I sigh as I lean back into the chaise. "That whole mess is definitely not something I want to get into right now."

"Speaking of messes, what the hell did Leni do to the room you're getting married in? It looks like Santa threw up in it."

"She's out of control. You know how she gets at Christmas." I shoot the other bottle of vodka and throw it in the trash can. "Do you remember when we used to go to Grandma's house the weekend before Christmas?"

"Yeah, she always mainlined us cookies, peppermint hot chocolate, and Christmas movies. It was seriously the best weekend of the year. I miss her so much."

"I wish Christmas could always be that chill. That's how I'm going to make mine and Steve's."

She rolls her eyes at me and sighs loudly. "Good luck with that."

"So are you going to take one more shot at talking me out

of getting married? It's T minus seventeen hours. You're cutting it pretty close."

"But who's counting, right?" She scoots her body across the floor and lays her head on my lap. "I'm not trying to talk you out of anything. If this is what you want, do it. But do it because your gut's telling you it's the right thing. And if your gut's telling you it's the wrong thing, let's leave right now and never look back."

"I think my gut's broken. It's been telling me one thing for two years, and now it's telling me something else," I say as I start untangling the knots in her curls. "I probably just have cold feet."

"Your gut's never been wrong. And every time you go against it, something bad happens." She pauses for a second and then starts laughing. "Do you remember when you jumped off that cliff into the rock quarry?"

"Do I remember? My foot still doesn't work right."

"You're lucky that's all you broke. I can still hear you hitting the water. It sounded so painful."

"Why did you let me do that?"

"Me? When have I ever been able to stop you from doing anything? If I could, we would have been out of this crazy sideshow yesterday."

"I'm getting married—"

"Okay. This is the last thing I'm going to say about it. The entire time we were growing up, your gut kept us out of a lot of trouble. But those few times you didn't listen to it, it was a complete disaster—broken bones, food poisoning, wrecked cars, and even school suspension. We could have avoided all of that. And as bad as it was, it's nothing compared to spending your life with someone you know isn't right. Whether he was right at one time doesn't matter. It only matters if he's the right one today—at this very moment."

We lock eyes. She knows. I know. We both know what my gut's telling me. I nod. She nods. She locks my pinky into hers.

"It's never too late," she whispers. I nod again.

"Let's get down to dinner," I say, standing and pulling her up with me. "We don't want to miss Mom's dress popping open when she takes her first bite of food."

Chapter Eight

NOELLE

December 21
Los Angeles, California

"I thought you changed your mind."

Steve laughs as he takes my arm and pulls me over to the head table. I inhale deeply. I wonder if he's starting to sense it, too. For months, I've thought that Steve's changing. He keeps telling me that it's just the stress of college ending, but it seems like something more. I've done a decent job of ignoring it, but now, at the last minute, it feels like there's a warning siren going off in my head.

He pulls out my chair and kisses me. That's about the end of our interaction for the next hour. We barely say anything to each other during the entire dinner. Between chatting with our wedding party and people stopping by the table to congratulate us, there's not a lot of couple time. The siren's getting louder. It's almost deafening now.

Someone taps the microphone. I look over to see Trip standing at the head of the room. Every eye in the room is locked on him before he even says a word. In addition to being very rich, he's outrageously good-looking. His thick, black hair is tinged with just the right amount of gray. Somehow he styles it so it looks magically wind-blown—one small curl always escaping the carefully managed waves. He has pale blue eyes that jump out of his olive skin. He's Irish on his dad's side, Greek on his mom's side. He's a stunning genetic combination of the two.

So far, I haven't really listened to one toast—not even from my maid of honor—but Trip's pulling me in as usual. He has an extraordinary ability to command a room—the small pauses to increase anticipation, the earnest eye contact with every person in the room, the hypnotically deep, calm voice. He's talking about family and loyalty and love. Even though I know he's full of it, I'm still completely engrossed until he drops an unexpected bomb.

". . . and that's why we're so excited that Steve and Noelle will be moving to Dallas right after their honeymoon."

Trip looks at us—his dazzling smile lighting up the room. Everyone claps including Steve. He's smiling back at his dad. I'm not sure what my face is doing, but it's definitely not smiling.

"We'll talk about it later," Steve says through clenched teeth. He doesn't take his eyes off his dad.

"Talk about what?" I whisper.

My face must be giving away my shock because Steve suddenly kisses me and then pulls me into a hug. There's more loud clapping and a few cat whistles from his groomsmen.

"Dad wants us to move to Dallas," he says into my ear as he holds me to him in a death grip. "I told him we'd think about it. Please don't cause a scene. We'll talk about it after dinner."

He lets go of my neck and kisses me softly one more time.

"To the happy couple!" I look back at Trip who's holding his champagne flute to the crowd. Everyone raises their glasses in unison, "The happy couple!" they exclaim—their eyes still fixed on Trip like he's the last ray of sunshine sinking below the horizon at sunset.

Steve forces a glass into my hand and clinks his glass with mine. He looks back at his dad. I look out in the crowd. Everyone's still looking at Trip except one person. Kit's wide eyes are fixed right on me. She tilts her head slightly toward the door as she starts to walk that way.

"I'm going to the restroom," I say to Steve. "And you're damn right we're going to talk about this. I'm not moving to Dallas."

He grabs my hand and tries to pull me back, but he's too late. I'm off the dais and headed toward the door. As I open it, Kit grabs my hand and pulls me into the kitchen.

"Dallas to L.A. is going to be a long commute every morning for class," she says as she pushes me into a tiny space behind the wine racks.

"I'm not moving to Dallas." I cover my face to muffle a scream.

"Did you tell Cary Grant? He seems to think you're moving."

I look up at her. "Oh my God. He does look like Cary Grant. Why did I never think of that?"

"That's your biggest question right now?"

"It's the only one my mind will let me process." I lean against the wall so I won't fall over. My body starts to shake.

Kit hugs me tightly. "Did Steve know?"

"Looks that way. He said we could talk about it after dinner."

"Well, that's big of him." She strokes my hair like Grandma used to do when I was upset. Kit's always reminded me of her. "What are you going to do?"

"I don't know." I start breathing like I'm trying to deliver a baby—pant, pant, blow, pant, pant, blow. "I need to talk to Steve. Will you get him?"

"Yeah, Elle. Just—"

"I know. I know. I'm focused on my gut now. I'm starting to think straight again. Just go get him, okay?"

She nods and disappears. A few minutes later, Steve charges through the door.

"Having Kit bring me to you. That's a little dramatic, don't you think?"

"Oh, you're about to see dramatic. Explain. Now!"

He rolls his eyes. "Dad needs help with the oil business, now that he's splitting his time between L.A. and Dallas. He asked if I'd start with the company after graduation."

"You're getting your MBA after graduation. And I'm going to law school. Or did you forget that?"

"I decided I didn't want to keep going to school. And you can go to law school in Dallas."

"I'm going to law school at Pepperdine, where I'm enrolled to start in January."

"Noelle, I think it's time for us to move on from California and be around family again."

"What are you even talking about right now? You've never said anything like this to me. And now you're springing it on me the night before our wedding?"

He puts his hand on my cheek. "As long as we're together, it shouldn't matter where we live."

I'm trying to think of how to reply to that when Trip walks in. He looks directly at me.

"Noelle, Steve just told me he hadn't talked to you about the move yet. That was a mistake. I'm sure you're just reacting to the quick change in plans, but Steve and I have been discussing this for months. I've already talked to the dean at the SMU law school. You can start there whenever you like, and we put an offer in for a house in University Park. You'll love it there. It's a little bohemian—like L.A. without the smog."

I'm too much in shock to say anything.

Trip continues. "Look, I know you love it out here where it's wild and free, but that was college. It's over now. It's time for both of you to grow up. You've had your playtime. Take a few more minutes, but then you need to come outside to thank our guests before they head out."

As he leaves, I look up at Steve. His eyes look tired. I swear he's aged five years in the last ten minutes. "Steve?"

"I made a mistake, okay? I should have talked to you about it. God, he has a way of hypnotizing me. We don't have to move if you don't want to."

"You made an offer on a house in Dallas."

"We can unmake it. It's fine. We'll stay here until you

finish law school and then talk about it some more. Maybe I can work at his production company out here."

He looks down at me. His lip's trembling. The only other time it's done that is when he was lying to me about making out with one of my sorority sisters.

"Let's go out and say goodbye to our guests," I say, starting toward the door. "And then I want to go to my room. I need some alone time."

Chapter Nine

NASH

December 22
Blitzen Bay, California

"My mom's making me go."

Gabi's just arrived with my breakfast. She puts the scrambled eggs and biscuits down and slides the ketchup bottle over to me.

"Nash, you're like six-foot-two, two hundred pounds," she says, laughing. "Are you still scared of your mommy?"

"One hundred percent. Do you think I'd be putting myself through this pain if I weren't?"

"Oh my God. Quit being such a baby. It's a wedding. You're not getting your teeth pulled."

"I'd rather be getting my teeth pulled," I grumble into my coffee.

Gabi plops down in the chair across from me. Her long, brown ponytail swings to one side. She raises her eyebrows and shakes her head slightly as she waits for me to give in—like I always do when she looks at me like this. I'm a little scared of her, too.

"I'm going, okay? I told Mom I would. I will. Leave me alone," I say, growling at her.

She laughs. She knows my bark is way worse than my bite. "Maybe you can even find a woman. You know weddings are chock-full of lonely, single women."

"Izzy! Come get your wife. She's annoying me." I look across the room. Izzy's petite body pops up from behind the bar.

"Nash, if I had to rescue everyone Gabi annoys, I'd be doing nothing but that all day."

Since I moved here, Gabi and Izzy have become my family. They saw the trauma in my eyes the first day I sat down in their bar. Despite my best efforts to avoid it, they adopted me on the spot. I moved here to get away from everyone. Now, I don't know what I'd do without them.

Izzy makes her way over to us. "If this guy hated you so much in high school, why did he invite you to his wedding? I think you're exaggerating."

"I never exaggerate." I slide the last corner of my biscuit across the plate to dab up the remaining gravy. "I don't know why he invited me. We played football together, but he's two years younger than me. I'm sure it has something to do with my mom. She's friends with his mom. Mom's always nagging me about getting out and meeting people."

"She's right. It wouldn't hurt you to get out of this town from time to time. You're not going to find a girlfriend here." Izzy picks up my empty plate and heads to the kitchen.

"I already have two girlfriends," I say to her retreating back.

"Who are married to each other," Gabi says. "You need to find a woman who prefers men."

"Why do I need to find a girlfriend at all? I'm fine the way I am."

Gabi pats my shoulder as she heads back to the bar. "You're not, but you keep believing that if it helps. Go to the wedding and find someone. At least find someone who you can spend the holidays with—it might cheer you up a little bit."

I grunt and check the time on my phone. It takes me an hour or so to get to L.A. If I'm going to this stupid wedding, I need to hustle. I throw a twenty on the table and move quickly toward the door.

"Nash! Quit leaving a twenty for an eight-dollar breakfast!" I hear Gabi yelling behind me.

The drive down to L.A. is torture. It's been exactly one year since Mikey died in front of me. It's all I can think about. There's no way being around people is a good idea right now. At every exit on the freeway, I think about turning around, but my brain won't let me.

I'm not sure why this wedding has gotten in my head this much. Ever since I got the invitation, it's been nagging at me —like an alarm that keeps going off. Every time I think about not going, my head feels like it's exploding. It's like I'm supposed to be there for some reason. I just can't imagine what that reason would be.

As I pull into the driveway, a parking attendant ushers me into a lot at the museum adjacent to the estate. He's trying to make me park in a tandem spot. I'm not about to get parked in. I drive over and park in a solo spot that has easy access to an escape route. The attendant hustles over to scold me, looks at my face, and walks away quickly.

I adjust the tie Hank gave me and put on his jacket. I shake my head to try to focus, and then follow the streams of people heading toward the mansion. As I walk in the front door, I hear a squeal coming from across the room.

"Nash Young! Your momma told me you were coming, but I said I wouldn't believe it until I saw you with my own two eyes."

I turn around to see Stevie's mom, Bitzy, charging across the room to me. She has on a shiny gold dress that would be too short on a toddler. The neckline plunges well below her very augmented chest. She looks like she's at a Las Vegas club instead of her son's wedding. She flips her long bleached hair behind her as she throws her body into mine. Her arms wrap too tightly around me as she rubs her cheek against my chest. She always was uncomfortably touchy.

"Mrs. Walker," I say as I pat her back a few times.

She takes one more squeeze and then pushes me back. "Let me take a look at you. Oh, still as handsome as ever. I thought you might have a crew cut since you just got out of the Army, but look how long your hair is, and with the beard, you look downright dangerous."

She reaches up to touch my beard, but I intercept and squeeze her hand while I gently lower it. "It's nice to see you, ma'am. Congratulations on the big day. My mom told me Stevie got a good one."

She puts both of her hands around her mouth like she's

forming a megaphone and whispers, "Well, between me and you, I think she's the one getting the catch. You know how the girls flock around Steve. He's always had his pick of the litter, but then you know what that's like. I'm sure you still have women falling at your feet."

"I do okay," I say, trying my best to smile. "Is Mr. Walker around? I'd like to say hi to him."

"Oh, who knows where he is? He's always off doing business somewhere. You'd think at his son's wedding, he could put down the phone for ten minutes, but no, there he is over there with it stuck to his ear." She flings her arms toward her newly located husband and then winks at me. "Well sweetie, you better find a seat. I'll find you at the reception. You owe me a dance."

She pats my butt as she walks away. I'm definitely leaving before that dance has a chance to happen. I'm not even sure I'm going to make it to the reception.

I see a group of people I went to high school with sitting on the left side of the aisle, so I duck my head and head over to the far right side. I take a seat next to an older couple who look like they won't want to talk. I glance at my watch—still thirty-five minutes until the wedding starts. I curse myself silently for arriving so early.

I think about leaving again. I wait for my brain to resist, but this time, it doesn't put up much of a fight. I feel like it's telling me 'Almost. Not quite, but it's almost time to go. Get ready.' I start shifting in my seat like a starter gun's about to go off. I'm ready to leave, brain, whenever you are. Just give me the signal.

DONNA SCHWARTZE

Chapter Ten

NOELLE

December 22
Los Angeles, California

"Mom, I don't think I can marry Steve."

My body's shaking like I'm sitting naked in the middle of a snowdrift. I'm actually sitting in my bridal suite dressed in my wedding gown. I'm getting married in thirty minutes.

"I'll marry him if you don't!" Carissa says too loudly. She's my maid-of-honor. She's always had a crush on Steve.

I look at my bridesmaids. For the first time, I realize they're all girlfriends of Steve's friends. Since we've been dating, I've lost touch with the friends I had before him. Why am I just realizing this?

My throat starts to close. I can't take a deep breath. My heart feels like it's about to burst through my chest. I've never had a panic attack, but I'm guessing this is the start of one.

"Girls, it's almost time!" Mom's voice is shrill. She ushers my bridesmaids out of the room. "Carissa, will you find Noelle's father? Tell him to come up here. It's almost time for him to walk his daughter down the aisle!"

They blow me kisses as they leave. "We'll see you down there, Noelle!"

Mom closes the door and turns around slowly. She's wearing a skintight, lace sheath dress. It's the brightest white I've ever seen. It's much whiter than my bridal gown.

"Refresh your lipstick, Noelle. It needs one more coat."

"Mom, didn't you hear me? I don't want to get married. I can't get married."

She walks over to me—each step more deliberate than the last—until she's standing inches from me. She tries to lean over to look me directly in the eyes, but her dress is too tight. Instead, she grabs my bare shoulder and pinches it.

"You're being dramatic again, Noelle. We've talked about it so many times. It's not necessary to use drama to get attention. Of course, you're getting married. And then you're moving to Dallas." She lets go of my shoulder and flings her arm in the air as she turns around. "Do whatever little yoga breathing you need to do to get yourself together. I'll be outside with your father."

When she closes the door, I walk over to lock it. My legs are shaking so hard I don't think they can support me anymore. I sink against the door. The dress's tight bodice digs into my ribs and makes it even harder to breathe. I feel like I'm about to pass out.

I slap my cheeks a few times to try to clear the panic that's swirling around in my head. I need to focus. I try to take a deep breath and start coughing uncontrollably. My eyes start to water. I crawl over to the makeup table to get a tissue.

I dab my eyes and throw it away. Something in the trash can catches my eye. The light's reflecting off a piece of glass. I brush away the tissue to reveal an empty vodka bottle from Kit's visit last night. Kit—that's who I need right now. I grab my phone.

My gut has never been wrong.

Just sending the text makes my breathing slow down a little bit.

It's never been wrong and it's not wrong now. You can't get married. Not to him.

She's right. I know it. She knows it. Mom probably even knows it. This marriage isn't right. I've known it for months. I wish I'd called it off with more than twenty-five minutes left on the clock, but it is what it is. This marriage is not going to happen. I know that for sure now. My head starts to clear, and my hands have almost stopped shaking.

I can't do this. Can you cause a scene? I need to escape.

My legs are working again. I look out the window. Kit broke the drain pipe away from the building when she climbed up here last night. There's no way I could shimmy down it with this dress on anyway. I need to change. I look around for some other clothes.

"Noelle, your father's coming up the stairs." Mom's voice sounds strained. "It's time."

She tries to open the door. She starts rattling the doorknob. There's no time to change my clothes. I have to go now. I need to get Mom away from the door. My phone beeps.

Can I cause a scene? Who do you think you're talking to?!! Just tell me when to start.

My body stops shaking. I look in the mirror. My eyes are telling me this is right.

Start now. And make it big. I need Leni to leave her post at my door.

I kick off my three-inch heels and slide into my flip-flops.

I'm on it. Don't take your phone. They can track it. This is the right decision. Call me when you can. I love you.

I press my ear to the door just in time to hear Mom scream. Her heels click across the room. As I crack the door, I see her back disappearing down the front stairs. I run in the opposite direction. I hear Kit's voice screaming "Jingle Bells." Mom hates that song. Kit and I used to sing it in rounds to annoy her.

I make it out of the room and down the back stairs without being seen. Apparently, everyone's left to see what's going on in the main room. I hear mom yelling, "Katherine! Get down off that stage now! Katherine! Give me the microphone!" Kit's

The Runaway Bride Of Blitzen Bay

voice gets louder. 'Jingle Bells! Jingle Bells! Jingle all the way.'

I open the exit door and see the parking lot in front of me. It's an endless field of getaway cars. It's too bad I don't have the keys to any of them. This is possibly the worst-planned escape ever. I have no idea where I'm headed—just somewhere other than here.

I make my way through the parked cars, dragging my long train with me. I told Mom I didn't want a train, but I ended up with something straight out of Princess Diana's wedding. I feel like I'm dragging a fifty-pound weight behind me. It's hampering my escape.

I'm only about a hundred feet away from the building when I hear Steve's voice. He's standing at the back door with his groomsmen. They're looking out at the parking lot, but luckily, I don't think they've seen me yet. I duck behind the SUV to my right and try to open the hatchback. It's locked. I look around until I see a truck with a tarp over its bed. It's worth a try.

Steve's voice gets louder. I open the truck's gate and shimmy headfirst under the tarp. I'm desperately trying to pull my train in with me when I see two hands shoving it the rest of the way into the truck bed and then closing the tailgate. I look through a crack between the tarp and the side of the truck and see a man with wavy, brown hair.

I'm about to say something to him when I hear Steve's voice—just inches from me. I throw my hands over my mouth.

"Nash Young," Steve says. His voice sounds sharp like it gets when I disagree with him. I can tell without seeing him that his teeth are clenched. "I couldn't believe when Mom told me you were coming to the wedding. I thought we'd lost you for good."

I look through the crack again. Steve's standing in front of my accomplice, whose name I guess is Nash. I've always thought Steve was a pretty big guy, but Nash towers over him.

"Stevie," Nash says as he leans back on the truck. "Did I look at the invitation wrong? Isn't your wedding about to start?"

Chapter Eleven

NASH

December 22
Los Angeles, California

"Are you a friend of the bride or groom?"

The old lady sitting next to me smiles as she pats my leg. I suddenly realize I've been shifting back and forth in my chair and probably hitting her.

"I went to high school with the groom," I say, smiling at her. "Sorry if I hit your chair. I'm kind of a restless person."

"No problem, dear. I'm a friend of the bride's grandma. She and I went to high school together many, many years ago. She was the sweetest woman. Noelle reminds me so much of her. She's much more like her grandma than her mom."

I smile and nod. I'm trying to think of something to say back to her when I see a woman with long blue hair walk to the lectern. She takes the microphone and starts singing "Jingle Bells" loudly and very off-key. She gestures wildly with her arms like she's playing to a packed house at the Hollywood Bowl.

She's screeching out the lyrics. It's more than I can take. I fulfilled my promise to Mom. I came to the wedding and now I'm leaving the wedding. My brain doesn't try to resist. Apparently, it's had enough, too.

When I get outside, I jog across the parking lot. Just as I'm getting in my truck, I catch a glimpse of something white and wispy disappearing behind a car about ten rows from me. At first, I think it might be a bird. It seems to be in distress.

I'm thinking about how I can help the poor thing when the white poof pops up again. It's not a bird. The poof's attached to a human head. The head looks around quickly and disappears. Then it pops up behind another car. I feel like I'm watching a really weird game of Whack-A-Mole.

The head gets closer to my truck and farther away from the building. When it gets within twenty feet of me, I recognize that the white poof is a bridal veil. The head rises just enough above the car that I can see it's attached to a woman wearing a wedding gown. I guess this is Stevie's bride, although what she's doing in the parking lot is not yet clear.

She makes her way behind another car and then freezes. She hears the voices I'm hearing. I look toward the building where I see a group of men in tuxedos looking out at the parking lot. Stevie's in the middle of them. He points out in the distance, but I don't think he sees her yet. I look back to her last location. She's gone. That's when I see movement in my rearview mirror. I duck down as I watch her open my tailgate and dive under the tarp that covers my truck bed.

I look up to see Stevie and his groomsmen getting closer. I

walk casually around to the back of my truck. Her dress is caught on the hitch. It starts to rip as she yanks at it. I unhook it and push the rest of the white fluff under the tarp. I'm just clicking the tailgate closed when the posse gets to my truck.

"Nash Young," Stevie says, trying to smile through clenched teeth. "I couldn't believe when Mom told me you were coming to the wedding. I thought we'd lost you for good."

"Stevie," I say, leaning back on the truck. "Did I look at the invitation wrong? Isn't the wedding about to start?"

A couple of his groomsmen laugh. Stevie lifts his hands and the laughing immediately stops. It looks like he still knows how to control his teammates with a quarterback's authority.

"Yeah, the wedding starts in a few minutes. You should get in there. We're just getting some fresh air before the ceremony." His lip starts to tremble. He's still a really bad liar.

"You're not thinking about running, are you?" I stare at him as he shifts uncomfortably. I could always stop him cold with just my eyes.

"Well, *he's* not thinking of running," one of the groomsmen says as they all break out laughing. "You haven't seen a bride anywhere, have you?"

Stevie whips around to look at them, but there's no controlling the obviously liquor-induced laughing.

"What's that mean?" I say as innocently as I can. "You lose your bride, Stevie?"

He takes a quick step closer to me—puffing out his chest. "Mind your own business, Nash. And I go by Steve now. You'd know that if you watch any college football."

"Yep. Steve Walker, UCLA's starting quarterback. Well, I mean until this year. That kid out of Fresno put you on the bench. Probably a good thing you're getting out, huh?"

"That's rich coming from someone who couldn't get past high school ball." He tries to stretch his barely six-foot frame up a little higher.

I smile. I'm done here. "Well, good luck with your hunt? I'm going in, so I can get a good seat for the big event."

Stevie glares at me as he walks away. His bottom lip's still trembling. That was always his tell when he was in over his head. I watch them turn the corner to the other parking lot before I open the tailgate. The dress spills out like a glacier melting in Antarctica.

"They're gone," I say as I sit on the tailgate.

There's no reply. I sit there for a minute. Still no reply. I whistle a few bars of "Here Comes The Bride." I hear some rustling under the tarp.

"That's not funny." She takes a deep breath and blows it out forcefully. More rustling.

"Just trying to get you to talk. You okay in there? I can take off the tarp so you can sit up."

Her hand darts out and grabs mine. "No! I don't want him to see me."

Even though she's almost squeezing the blood supply out of my hand, I can't help but notice how silky and soft her hand feels. I put my other hand on top of it.

"They've gone around the building. No one's here except for us," I say as I squeeze her hand gently between mine. She doesn't say anything, but she squeezes my hand back. I try again. "I can't imagine you're too comfortable and you're probably getting your dress dirty. Let me help you out."

"I'm not coming out." She pulls her hand back underneath the tarp. "Please don't tell him I'm here. I know you're friends, but just let me stay here for a minute."

"You can stay there as long as you want. And I'm not Stevie's friend."

"You played football with him in high school, right?"

"Yeah, doesn't mean we're friends though."

"He invited you to our wedding."

I bend down to look under the tarp. I only see a jumble of white material, but I know she has to be in there somewhere. "Do you really want to argue about how strong my relationship is with him? I think the strength of your relationship might be more in question right now."

The white material starts shifting around. Suddenly, her head pops out. She looks up at me. I stop breathing for a second. She's beautiful. She has soft blonde hair and light brown eyes. Her skin's as ivory and delicate as her dress. I have an overwhelming urge to touch it. I look away quickly.

"Your name's Nash?"

"Yeah."

"He's never talked about you."

"Not surprising. What's your name? I saw it on the invitation, but I'm forgetting. Something Christmas-y."

"Noelle."

"That's it. You must have been born in December."

"August 12. My mom insisted I have a Christmas name for some reason."

"I'm guessing your mom insists on a lot of things. Like

maybe you getting married?" I look back down at her. Her eyes are closed. The sun's reflecting off the glitter on her eyelids.

"I don't want to talk about it. Will you just get me out of here?"

"Get you out of here?" I sit up straight. "Like leave your wedding?"

"Yes. As far away as possible. Please." She opens her eyes. They're sparkling at me. I'm pretty sure she can hypnotize people with them. I look away again.

"Maybe you should talk to Steve?"

"You promised you wouldn't tell him I'm here." She puts her hand on my leg. A warm, tingly feeling shoots through my body.

"And I'm not going to." Her hand's still on my leg. It's distracting me. I look over my shoulder to make sure we're still alone. Mr. Walker's standing outside on his phone, but he's too far away to see us. "I'm just saying maybe you should tell him what's going on in your head right now."

"I'm not even sure what's going on in my head right now. I just know I have to get out of here. Will you please take me somewhere?"

I inhale deeply and exhale through my teeth. I know this is a bad decision, but it's clear my brain's not in charge of my body right now. "Fine. Where would you like to go?"

"I can't go anywhere they know about. Will you take me to where you're staying? I need to find a place to call my cousin. She'll pick me up."

"I live up in the mountains. It's like an hour's drive from

here. Why don't we get you upfront? I'll drive you to a private place away from here. You can use my cell to call her."

She scoots back under the tarp. "I can't get out. Someone will see me. Just drive and stop somewhere down the road."

"All right," I say as I take off Hank's jacket. "It's going to get cold back there. At least put this on."

Her hand pulls the jacket under the tarp. Some of her hair's still draped over the tailgate. I gently gather it in my hand and place it inside the truck bed. It feels even silkier than her hand. I'm frozen in place. My body doesn't want to move. I have an overwhelming urge to crawl under the tarp with her. I shake my head to try to wake up my brain.

I take another deep breath and gently close the tailgate. "Hold on. You're probably in for kind of a bumpy ride."

I hear her sigh and whisper, "You have no idea."

Chapter Twelve

NOELLE

December 22
Los Angeles, California

"What the hell were you thinking?" I whisper as the truck starts moving.

This is maybe the worst idea I've ever had. How bad does the situation have to be when escaping your wedding in the back of a stranger's truck feels like the best option?

My gut's telling me this was the right choice. I think it might be broken though. I mean, what if this Nash guy doesn't stop the truck? What if he keeps driving to Mexico or something? For all I know, he's going to kidnap me and take me for his bride.

I close my eyes to try to center my thoughts. Lola pops into my mind. She always tells me a person's energy doesn't lie. Nash has a calming energy. I could sense it immediately. He smiled at me so warmly that it almost melted the iceberg of stress that's lodged in my chest. And when he put his hands around mine, my body relaxed like it does when I hear the ocean rippling onto the shore.

Of course, it doesn't hurt that he has beautiful soft-green eyes. And why did I have the urge to run my fingers through his messy brown curls? I need to get it together. I just left one man at the altar. This is no time to be thinking about another one, especially a total stranger.

My teeth chatter as the wind pours through the cracks between the tarp and the sides of the truck. I pull his jacket over my face. It smells so good—kind of like cedar trees and soap. I want to sniff his hair to see if it smells like that, too. Steve's hair always smells like my shampoo. He uses more of it than I do.

Steve. Yes. That's who I should be thinking about. I feel so guilty. He's not a bad guy. I loved him. Or do I still love him? Did I ever love him? I'm not even sure right now. I just know marrying him today was not the right thing to do. Maybe, I should have talked to him instead of running away, but I felt like an animal trapped in a corner. Everyone was moving in on me. I had to fight my way out.

Mom's going to kill me—like I think she might literally kill me. She would definitely think it was justifiable. I know she's screaming right now—at no one in particular—just screaming. Even though we're at least a mile down the road, I swear I can hear her.

And Dad. Poor Dad. He's probably hiding somewhere—from Mom and the world. When the drama starts, he always hides and lets Mom deal with the fallout.

I know I've disappointed everyone—well, everyone except

me. Even though my mind's still racing, my body finally feels calm. Once Kit picks me up, she'll help me figure out what to do next. The only thing I know for sure is that I'm staying in California and I'm going to law school. Everything and everyone else needs to fit into that picture.

Now, I have to figure out how to get out of my current predicament. He's driving really slowly. I wonder if I can open the tailgate and roll out. I think the bulk of my dress would probably protect me from injury.

As I'm considering my options, the truck stops. I hear him open his door. The panic starts to rise in my body again. I pull his jacket over my head—hoping I'll disappear.

"You still in there?" I hear him say as he starts unhooking the tarp.

I hold my breath and close my eyes tightly.

Chapter Thirteen

NASH

December 22
Los Angeles, California

"What the hell were you thinking?" I say to myself as I drive slowly down the winding canyon road.

I'm just starting to realize what's happening. Somehow, I let a strange woman convince me to smuggle her out of her wedding. And I'm driving through L.A. with her trapped in the back of my truck. I can hear my defense attorney telling me no one on the jury will believe she asked me to take her. And frankly, I would agree with them.

I'm not sure why I didn't pull her out of my truck and drive away. Why have I made this my problem? I swear she hypnotized me. I'm not thinking clearly at all. There's something about her that hit me deeply—like an overwhelming need to protect her. I want to wrap my arms around her and take away all of her stress. I need to snap out of it. That's not going to happen. I have to get rid of her as quickly as possible. I see an empty parking lot and pull into it.

I walk around the back of the truck. It's so quiet I think she might have slipped out somewhere along the way. That would solve all of my problems, but for some reason, it makes me start to panic.

"You still in there?" I say as I unclasp the pulleys holding the tarp on the truck bed. I pull it back to reveal a mound of wedding dress with Hank's jacket in the center of it. I think for a second that she's disappeared, but as I carefully lift the jacket, two eyes pop out of a mess of blonde hair.

"I'm so cold," she says, sitting up suddenly. Her hair falls in disorganized clumps onto her bare shoulders. Her veil's barely clinging to one side of her head. She looks like a little kid playing dress-up in her mom's closet.

"I told you it would be cold back here," I say, reaching for her hand. "C'mon. Let's get you warmed up."

She grabs the top of her strapless dress and shimmies a few times as she pulls it a little farther back up. "Strapless dresses are a pain. Don't let anyone tell you differently."

"I definitely won't."

She tries a few times to stand but keeps catching her feet in the dress. Then she tries to crawl over to me, but her dress is caught on something. She finally falls back into the layers of silk.

"Maybe I should just take it off." She reaches around her back to start unzipping.

"No!" I move quickly around to the side of the truck. The

The Runaway Bride Of Blitzen Bay

last thing I need is to see more of her. What I'm seeing is already tempting enough. I add, "You're not going to get warmer by taking clothes off. I think it's going to be easier if I lift you out."

I unhook the piece of material that's snagged on the side of the truck and place my hand hesitantly on her bare back.

"You ready?" I say to warn her that I'm about to grab her.

When I get her into my arms, she looks up at me—her eyes wide and a sweet smile on her full lips. I want to kiss her so badly.

"Are you okay? Is my dress still caught?" She looks back at the truck bed long enough for me to snap out of my daydream.

"No, I think we're all good." I look away from her and toward the truck. "Hey, will you open the door?"

I place her down on the seat gently and hand her the jacket. She wraps it around her shoulders. Her dress is still spilling out of the truck. I start piling it on top of her.

"I think this dress probably weighs more than you do."

She laughs as she gathers it onto her lap. "The train was my mom's idea. I wanted something simple."

I look up at her. She's watching me. Her eyes are soft and inviting. I hand her the last of the dress. When her hand brushes over mine, a wave of electricity surges through me.

When I get around the back of the truck, I look at her again. It looks like she's turned the heat on full blast. It's blowing her veil all over the place. She's struggling to detach it from her head. I think back to what Sam said about his wife bringing calm to his chaos. What did I tell him? That I was the calm one, so I needed to find 'the female version of chaos.' Her veil has wrapped around her head. She's swatting at it. It looks like she's fighting a flock of birds. Frankly, it looks like complete chaos.

Chapter Fourteen
NOELLE

December 22
Los Angeles, California

"Are you warming up at all?"

When he gets in the truck, I have the heat on its highest level. I'm still shaking. He points his vents toward me.

"Yeah." I throw my veil on the dashboard and wrap his jacket tighter around me. "I guess I should have thrown on a sweater or something before my escape."

"Escape, huh? That usually means someone was holding you against your will." He looks up at me. His soft eyes are suddenly very hard. "Anything you want to tell me?"

"They were holding me, but mentally only." I turn from him and look out the window. "It's a long story."

"Okay. Here's my phone if you want to call your cousin. Do you know her number?"

"Yeah, it's one of only two I have memorized." I take the phone from him and dial Kit. She answers immediately.

"Elle?" She's whispering. I can barely hear her.

"Yeah, it's me." For some reason, I'm whispering, too.

"Where are you? Are you okay?"

"Yeah. Some guy gave me a ride. I'm fine."

"Some guy? What guy?"

"He's a high school friend of Steve's."

"What? Why would Steve's friend help you run away from him? Is he a kidnapper or something? Put me on speaker."

I turn to Nash who's looking out his window—trying his best not to eavesdrop. "You're on speaker. My cousin wants to know if you're a kidnapper."

He whips his head around to look at me. "You crawled into my truck and begged me to get you away from your wedding. How am I a kidnapper in this situation?"

"It doesn't mean you're not a kidnapper," Kit yells. "Maybe you're just a kidnapper who got lucky."

"Oh, yeah, I feel like the luckiest man on earth right now."

"What? Elle, he's sarcastic! You know how I love that."

"Yeah, and he's kind of grumpy, too. It's really cute."

"Stop!" Kit yells and then lowers her voice back down to a whisper. "Now is not the time to be crushing on a man."

"No, not cute like that. Cute like in a best friend kind of way."

Nash shakes his head, looking from the phone to me. "So now, I'm your best friend? We've known each other for twenty minutes."

"I'm her best friend, kidnapper. Settle down," Kit says.

"What's your name, by the way? So I can send the FBI after you if needed."

"Nash Young. Please send the FBI directly to me, so I don't have to talk to you two anymore."

"Aww, Elle, he's willing to go to federal prison for us. That's the first guy who's offered that."

"Are you forgetting about the guy in Key West?" I say, turning the heat down a notch. I'm finally starting to warm up.

"Yeah, but he went to normal prison. Kidnapper's offering to go to federal prison. It's special. He's a keeper."

"No, I'm not a keeper. At all." Nash picks the phone up off my lap and puts it on the dashboard. "I don't want to be kept by either of you. Will you please come and get your cousin?"

"Wait, where are you?" Kit says, whispering again.

"We're about a mile or so from the venue. He pulled over so I could call you."

"No, Elle, bad idea. They're looking for you. You need to get far away from here. Kidnapper, will you keep her? Just for a few hours or so."

"So, now you want me to kidnap her?" Nash groans and rubs his hands over his face.

I put my hand on his shoulder. "Well, maybe less like kidnapping and more like inviting a friend over to your house to chill for a few hours."

He shakes his head. "We're not friends."

"Wow. Okay. Rude."

"So rude." Kit chimes in. "Oh damn, Leni's making a beeline for me. I've got to go. I'll call you on this phone when I'm clear."

The phone goes dead. Nash looks at me—his mouth wide

open. He throws his hands up. "So now you're coming home with me? Will you please call Steve and work this out?"

"I don't know his number."

"That's not the other number you have memorized?" He's so exasperated. It's adorable.

"No. It's to the sushi place down the street from my apartment." He's squinting like he's trying to figure out how to kill me without going to jail. "3-1-0-C-A-L-R-O-L-L, like California Roll. It's cute, right?"

He shakes his head again and starts massaging his temples. "Here's what's going to happen. I'm driving you to Blitzen Bay—where I live—and getting you a room at the inn there. Then you're on your own."

He maneuvers the truck back onto the road.

"You live in a place called Blitzen Bay? Are you making that up?"

"No." He's looking away, trying his best to ignore me.

"Blitzen like the reindeer? Nash, do you live in a town named after a reindeer? Because that would be so precious."

"It's named after the German word for lightning," he says, looking at me sternly. "Blitz. Lightning. No one would name a town after a reindeer."

"Well, I mean, not an average reindeer, but I think Blitzen was Rudolph's dad, so he could probably get a town named after him."

"It's not named after a reindeer." He turns to me. "You know you seem pretty happy for a woman who just left her fiancé at the altar."

I take a deep breath and look away from him. "Not happy. I

guess more relieved than anything. And my adrenaline's still pumping from the escape. I'm going to crash once my brain catches up with what I've just done. I think it's going to get ugly."

His voice gets softer. "You'll be fine. Pretty women can get away with anything."

"Aww, Nash. Do you think I'm pretty?"

"You know you're pretty, although I can't say you look all that great right now."

"How dare you!" I cover my chest with my hand. "And on my wedding day."

He laughs. "That look won't work on me at all, but I'm sure it made your dad think you were innocent more than once."

I grab his rearview mirror and turn it toward me. "He knew darn well I wasn't innocent. Do you mind if I use your mirror?"

"Well, you know, it comes in handy for things like driving, but knock yourself out."

I start taking bobby pins out of my hair and throwing them on his dashboard. "My dad just wanted peace in the house. I could have robbed a bank and as long as I didn't get caught, he wouldn't have cared."

"I can appreciate that. Peace is underrated. That's all I want. It's the reason I moved to California. I just want to be alone."

"Yeah? How's that working for you today?" I look over at him again. He's trying not to laugh.

"Not too good. I had almost escaped to peace when a crazy woman crawled into the back of my truck."

"Wait. What do you mean escape? Were you going into the wedding or were you leaving?"

"I was at the wedding when some lady with blue hair started singing "Jingle Bells." It was the worst thing I've ever heard. I couldn't take it anymore."

"That was my cousin Kit!" I say, pointing to his phone. "She was creating a diversion for me so I could escape."

"You mean she wasn't a planned part of the wedding?"

"No! Do you think I'd have someone sing "Jingle Bells" at my wedding? I'm not crazy."

"All evidence to the contrary."

"Funny," I say as I throw one of my bobby pins at him.

"I thought you were really into Christmas. Like all the lights and that big life-sized Santa . . . I don't think "Jingle Bells" is much of a stretch from there."

"The decorations are all my mom. She's the crazy one. My idea of a perfect Christmas is much more chill than that."

"I don't believe you have a chill bone in your body."

I sigh. "You'd be surprised. My favorite part of Christmas was snuggling on the couch with my grandma, watching movies, and drinking peppermint hot chocolate."

"That sounds more my speed." He looks over at me and sees the tear rolling down my cheek. He reaches over to pat my hand. "Maybe you can do that with your grandma this year. Might make you feel better."

"She died four years ago."

"Oh man, Elle, I'm so sorry."

I wipe the tear away and smile at him. "Wait. Did you call me Elle?"

"Yeah. Sorry. I have this thing about shortening people's names. Bad habit. I meant Noelle."

"You can call me Elle. There are only two people who call me that and they're two of my favorite people ever created—Kit and my grandma. Now three of my favorite people call me that."

He raises his eyebrows and laughs. "Now I'm your best friend and one of your favorite people?"

"Well, it would be silly if my best friend wasn't one of my favorite people."

He shakes his head and looks back toward the road. A slight smile comes to his lips. I rest my head against the window. For the first time in months, my body feels completely relaxed.

Chapter Fifteen

NASH

December 22
Blitzen Bay, California

"This is the road into Blitzen Bay."

I'm not sure if she's asleep. After she talked about her grandma, she closed her eyes and laid her head against the window. She's been quiet for about ten minutes. I'm guessing that's a record for her.

She sits up and looks out the front window. Walls of rock surround us on both sides where they cut the road through the mountain. She lays her head on the dashboard and looks up.

"You ever been up there?" She cranes her neck a little farther.

"I don't think there are roads that go up to the top. This is the only road that goes into this area of the mountain—one road in, one road out."

"Huh," she says, sitting back. "Kind of like *Seven Brides for Seven Brothers*."

"I have no idea what that is."

"You've never seen *Seven Brides for Seven Brothers*?"

"Is it a movie?"

"Yeah." She pulls her legs up to her chest and lays her head on her knees. "It's a great movie. It's about seven brothers who kidnap seven brides—well potential brides—because they want to marry them."

"So, it's like a crime drama?"

"No, it's a musical."

"There's a musical about kidnapping?" I look over at her. She's peeking at me from under her long, blonde curls that are now flowing over her shoulders.

"You don't get it," she says, pushing some of it behind her ear. "I mean, the women like the men. They want to marry them."

"Then why do the men have to kidnap them?"

"Stop! You're getting me off my original point."

"There's a point to this?"

"Yes! There was only one road to the men's house—just like this. They caused an avalanche so the women couldn't be rescued until spring."

"So now, it's a movie about kidnapping and imprisonment? And they sing about it?"

"Sing and dance. There's one really cool musical number with sawhorses."

I look at her, squinting my eyes. "You're making this up, right?"

"No! It's a great movie. You should watch it."

"Yeah, that's not going to happen. And just so we're clear, there's not enough snow in this area to cause a road-blocking avalanche, so you can leave whenever you want. In fact, I can take you back right now."

She rolls her eyes and looks back out the front windshield as we're cresting the hill that leads down into the valley. The sun's jagged rays are reflecting off the snow flurries that have just started to swirl.

"Is this Blitzen Bay?" she says, looking at me with her eyes wide.

"Yeah. Pretty, huh?"

She looks back down to the valley. "It looks like a snow globe. It's beautiful."

I drive down Main Street and pull up in front of Izzy's.

"One of the owners of this bar is about your size if you want to change your clothes."

"Yes, please." She grabs the door handle. "I can't wait to get into something comfortable."

I grab her arm and pull her back. "Wait for me to come around and get you. I don't want you to fall in the snow. With that dress on, I might not ever find you."

She's putting flip flops back on her feet when I open her door. I shake my head.

"They made more sense when we were in L.A.," she says, trying to jump down.

I stop her. "Nope. You're going to get frostbite on your feet. I'll carry you."

When we walk into the bar, everyone stops talking. I'm just realizing what this looks like. I'm carrying a bride over the threshold into the room.

"Seriously?" Gabi says, peering at me from behind the bar. "I tell you to find a single woman at the wedding and you bring home the bride?"

She puts her hands on the bar and leans forward so she can get a better look at the billows of white falling all around Elle.

"Well technically, she's still single." I usher Elle over to a seat at the far end of the bar. "You think Izzy has any clothes she can wear? They're about the same size, right?"

"Honey, are you okay?" Gabi strolls over and pats Elle's hand. "Blink twice if he's holding you against your will."

She smiles as she squeezes Gabi's hand. "I'm fine. Actually, I think I might be holding him against his will."

"Hmm." Gabi turns to me. "Are you making her say that?"

I roll my eyes at her as Izzy charges through the kitchen door.

"Wait, what's this I'm hearing? Does Nash have a lady friend with him?" She wipes her hands on her apron before she extends one to Noelle. "Hi. I'm Gabi's wife, Isabelle, and I can already feel in your aura that you're the perfect person for Nash."

"Better take a look at what's she's wearing before you make any more predictions, honey," Gabi says, laughing.

Elle smiles and shakes Izzy's hand. "Nice to meet you. I'm Noelle and I could really use a change of clothes. Do you have anything I can borrow?"

Gabi pushes Izzy out from behind the bar as Elle slides Hank's jacket off and hands it to me. Izzy laughs when she sees the wedding dress. "Only you, Nash. Did you tackle her halfway down the aisle and run off with her?"

"I didn't kidnap her! Why does everyone think I'm a caveman all of a sudden?"

"Well, I don't know about 'all of a sudden.'" Izzy takes Elle's arm and pulls her toward the back stairs that lead up to her apartment.

"Wait." I stand up and walk toward them. "Elle, come here for a second."

She follows me over to the corner of the room and frowns when she sees my serious face. "What's wrong?"

"You need to call Steve. I know he's worried about you."

"You don't even like him. Why do you care what he's feeling?"

"I don't like him—at all. But you apparently love him or did at one time." I put my hand on her shoulder. "Did he hurt you or something?"

She shakes her head. "No, nothing like that. It's just—"

"Stop. You don't have to explain it to me. I'm just saying if you were my bride—no matter what hideous thing I did to make you want to run away from me on our wedding day—I would still be worried until I knew you were safe."

She looks down at her feet and sighs. "You're right."

"I'm what?" I take an exaggerated step back. "Could you maybe say it louder so the whole room can hear?"

She whips her head back and smiles.

"No one likes a know-it-all, Nash. Stop being obnoxious," she says loudly as she walks back over to Izzy.

"Look at that! She just met you and she already has you figured out." Izzy smiles broadly and blows me a kiss as they start up the stairs. As the door closes, I hear her say, "Okay, bride. Start talking. I want to know everything."

"Izzy! Leave her alone," I say to the closed door. "She's already had a rough day."

I turn back around to see Gabi grinning at me. "Are you going to tell me the story? Or do I have to wait for Iz to tell me? You know she's not letting that girl leave our apartment until she knows every last detail."

"Yeah. And everyone thinks I'm the kidnapper," I sigh. "Can I please get a beer—or five? It's been a weird day."

She slides a bottle over to me. "Do you know what liquor your bride likes? Or should I wait for her to come back down?"

"I barely know her name. She got in the back of my truck to hide from the groom. And then asked me to take her away from her wedding."

"Before or after she said 'I do'?"

"Before. She's not married. She ran away before that happened. Or I guess I took her away," I say, quickly adding, "Not by force. She begged me to get her out of there and for some reason I did. I have no idea what I was thinking."

"Oh, I have some idea what you were thinking." Gabi laughs as she hands me another beer. "She's beautiful."

"I wasn't thinking that—at all. I don't have much interest in a woman who's so screwed up she has to flee her wedding day in the back of my truck."

"Much. You don't have 'much interest.'" She smiles as she walks to the other side of the bar. "You know you can't hide anything from me. I saw the way you were looking at her."

My eyes follow her across the room. She's getting refills for Hank and Claire. They wave at me as I head over to them.

"Hey Hank, Claire. My friend," I say, gesturing toward the

apartment door, "might need a place to stay tonight. You have any openings?"

Hank pushes his empty to Gabi. "We have one room left and it's all yours, Nash. I guess your house is still a little too rough to host a lady, huh?"

"No! I'm not staying with her," I say. "I need the room just for her. Alone. Not with me."

"He's cute when he's flustered," Claire says, looking at me as she sips her fresh glass of wine.

"I don't think I've ever seen him like this." Gabi finishes Hank's drink and hands it to him. "Nash, I think you might be blushing."

"I'm not blushing," I growl. "I don't have any interest in her. It's not like that."

"Oh, I think it's exactly like that," Claire says. "I might have to guard her room tonight, so you don't steal her away and marry her yourself."

"Ooh, like Milly had to guard the girls in *Seven Brides for Seven Brothers*."

I slam my bottle down on the bar. "Are you being serious right now? Did Elle tell you to say that?"

Gabi pats my hand. "I met her five minutes ago and you heard every word she said to me."

"She was just going on about that movie when we were driving in here. She said the pass reminded her of the avalanche or something."

Claire gasps. "Oh my God, it kind of does. I've never thought of that. Who knows, Nash? Maybe you'll get to keep her until spring."

Claire and Gabi burst out laughing.

Hank looks at me. "Do I want to know?"

"It's some movie about seven guys kidnapping seven girls . . ."

He nods. "Hmm. Sounds interesting. Do any of them escape or do most of them die?"

Claire and Gabi both collapse on the bar—their bodies shaking with laughter.

"Apparently all they do is sing and dance."

Hank looks at me like I'm high. I put my hand up to stop him before he can say anything more.

"Don't try to understand it. It's not worth your time. Believe me. I'll let you know if we need the room."

I grab my beer and start back over to my stool. When I whip around, Claire and Gabi are holding their breath.

"I mean she! I'll let you know if she needs the room —not we."

"I'm definitely sleeping outside her room, Nash," Claire says as she collapses down on the bar again.

Chapter Sixteen

NOELLE

December 22
Blitzen Bay, California

"Well, now that outfit is a little less conspicuous."

Gabi looks up as I come back through the door into the bar. I have on a pair of Izzy's jeans, an off-white fisherman's sweater, and hot pink fuzzy socks.

Nash looks down at my feet as I walk over.

"Her shoes are too little for me," I say as I slide onto the barstool next to him. "At least these are warmer than my flipflops."

"We have a general store here. They sell everything from boots to bird food. We'll get you fixed up when they open tomorrow," he says and then looks up at me. "I mean if you end up staying tonight."

I smile at him as Gabi walks over to us. "I bet the bride could use a large glass of liquor. What's your drink?"

"Vodka soda," I say, exhaling slowly. "Please."

"Absolutely not. That's a stupid drink."

"Gabi! Be nice. Give her what she wants," Nash says.

"Nope. Noelle, have you ever tried a Madras? Izzy and I drank those on our honeymoon."

"She's not on her honeymoon, Gabi—"

I grab Nash's arm. "It's fine. Whatever you want to serve me, just give me a double shot."

"I've got you covered," Gabi says, turning her back to us as she grabs a glass and fills it with ice.

Nash is staring at me. His eyes are seriously the prettiest green color I've ever seen. My knee touches his as I turn to face him. I don't move it.

"I called Steve. He's on his way up here."

He jumps a little bit and moves his knee away from mine.

"That's good," he says, looking back at Gabi. "Did you change your mind about the wedding?"

"I don't know that I changed my mind, but you were right. I need to talk to him. And I don't want my family worrying about me."

"That's sensible. I'm glad you called him. Is he mad?"

"Uh, I'm not sure, but my mom is. She was screaming in the background. I told Steve he had to come alone. I can't deal with her right now."

"Moms have a way of taking over, don't they?" he says, laughing. "My mom's the only reason I went to your wedding. She bullied me into it."

"Thank God for her or I never would have had a getaway driver."

Gabi slides a drink over to me that looks like a sunset—

oranges and reds swirling around the white liquor. "It's a double shot of vodka with a splash of OJ, cranberry, and lime. You want anything to eat?"

"I'm starving. I haven't eaten anything since early this morning. But I won't have any money until Steve gets here—"

"Stop," Nash says, finally turning back to me. "I'm paying. I'm hungry, too. They have the best cheeseburgers if you eat that."

"Yes, please, with a mound of fries." I take a long drink and look at Nash. "Hey. Do you mind if we grab a table? I need to lean on something. I feel exhausted all of a sudden."

"Yeah. Of course." He grabs his beer and my drink and gestures for me to go ahead of him. He follows me over to a table in the corner.

As he puts the drink in front of me, I take his wrist. "Nash, thank you for everything you've done today. Really. You've been so sweet. You have no idea how much this means to me. I owe you."

"You don't owe me anything. Just be happy. Figure out what that is and be happy." He squeezes my hand as he sits down.

I lean back in my chair. "So Izzy told me you just retired from the Army. You were a Ranger, huh?"

"Izzy talks too much. Don't tell her anything you don't want everyone else to know."

"I'm afraid I pretty much told her everything already," I say, tilting my head and smiling. "And you didn't answer my question."

"And I'm not going to, because I don't know you and it's

none of your business." He smiles before he drains the last of his beer. "And I told you that look doesn't work on me."

"Hmm." I sip on my drink as I sit back.

"I'm sorry Izzy interrogated you."

"It doesn't bother me. I'm an open book."

"Oh, okay." He leans back and strokes his beard. "If you're such an open book, tell me why you left Stevie at the altar."

My head jerks back a little like someone slapped me.

"Wow, okay, I guess I don't have any problem telling you that," I say slowly, "if you'll answer a question for me."

"No deal. I don't want to answer questions, but you're the one saying you're an open book, so why the hesitation?"

I lay my chin on my hands and fix my eyes on him. "I am an open book, but I also believe in fair play. I'll answer that question, but you have to answer one of mine."

He sits back and crosses his arms. "You can ask me a question about anything except my military service."

"Nope, no banned subjects."

He squints his eyes. "Ask, but I have the right to refuse any question."

"How old were you when you became a Ranger?"

"You're assuming what Izzy told you was accurate and that I was a Ranger—"

"We both know it is. How old? I'm not asking you to reveal military secrets."

"Nineteen."

"Wow! That's young." I sit up straighter.

"Not really. You can start the school at eighteen if you pass all the testing. And don't think I didn't notice you asked another question."

I put my hands up defensively. "I did not ask another question. I made a statement and you volunteered further information."

He shakes his head as he starts to laugh. "Your turn. Start answering."

"I left Steve at the altar because I didn't have the balls to break it off months ago when I should have." I look up at the ceiling. "And I feel horrible about it."

He reaches out and puts his hand on top of mine. "Why did you want to break it off in the first place?"

"That's a second question, but I'll allow it," I say, smiling. "It's kind of hard to explain. The entire time I was growing up, I felt like I was in a cage. People telling me what to do and who to be. And everything they wanted me to be didn't seem right. When I moved to L.A., it felt like someone opened the cage. I started finding little bits of myself I didn't know existed and when I started putting them all together, I was a different person—a person I really liked."

"And Stevie didn't like that person?"

"He did at first. I met him before my junior year. He was fun and free and he seemed like the kind of person I was trying to be. But as we got closer to graduation, he started reverting to the guy I guess he was before college. It's like he just took a break to play and have fun, but for me it was real. The person I grew into in college was who I wanted to be. Does that make sense?"

"Yeah, people grow apart all the time."

"It's more than that though. I realized the Steve I fell in

love with didn't even exist. It was like a role he was playing and the role was coming to an end."

"I'm sorry," he says, patting my hand. "That had to be a shock when you realized it."

"I wish I'd figured it out sooner, but I guess I'm lucky I figured it out before it was too late."

"So, are you going to give him another chance to work it out?" His gentle green eyes are suddenly hard and unblinking.

Izzy arrives with our dinner just in time for me to avoid answering that question.

"What are you doing telling her my secrets, Iz? You need to keep that mouth shut." He hands her his empty beer bottle.

"Oh, sweetie, I wasn't even close to telling her your secrets. I don't want to scare her," Izzy says, patting him on the shoulder. She looks at me. "You want a refill?"

"Yes, please. And keep them coming."

I grab a handful of fries and put them on my plate. He's staring at me.

"What? Do you not want me using my hands?"

"You didn't answer my last question." He grabs fries from the plate with his hand—his eyes still firmly fixed on me.

"And I'm not going to because I barely know you and it's none of your business," I say, laughing.

"Okay, open book, whatever you say."

He smiles as he picks up his cheeseburger. The way he's looking at me sends goosebumps up and down my body. I look down at my plate quickly.

Chapter Seventeen

NASH

December 22
Blitzen Bay, California

"So why did you hate Steve in high school?"

Elle looks up at me as she drags a French fry through the ketchup on her plate.

"I didn't hate him. Not really. We just weren't good friends, you know? I'm two years older than him to start with."

"Wow, I didn't know you were that old," she says, tapping her lips with her index finger.

"Settle down," I say, shaking my head. "You're only two years younger than me."

"I'm four years younger than you. I turn twenty-three next year."

"Ahh, I thought you were Steve's age."

"Nope. He was on the six-year college plan."

"That's right." I stroke my beard—my habit when I'm trying to remember something. "I forgot he redshirted his first two years in college."

"I don't know what that means, but yeah, he's two years older than me."

"Damn," I say, sighing. "You're a baby."

"I make up for it with my advanced maturity." She takes a sip of her drink and narrows her eyes. "I still don't get why he invited you to our wedding."

"He probably invited most of the guys from the football team. We ran around together."

"Oh, that explains it," she says, nodding. "He talks about his high school team a lot. Did he play quarterback there, too?"

"Yeah, and it seems like you should know that."

"I barely know what he played in college. I'm not much of a sports fan."

"That's blasphemy. How did you grow up in Georgia and not like sports?"

"There are other things to do in Georgia."

"What things?" She looks at me mischievously. "Wait. Stop. I don't think I want to know."

"You probably don't. Kit and I got into our share of trouble. Did you want to play football in college?"

I push my chair back a bit as I polish off my second cheeseburger. "I had quite a few scholarship offers, but I didn't want to keep going to school."

"So you went into the Army?"

"Yeah, and oddly, I studied more there than I probably would have in college."

She nods. "I bet Ranger school was tough."

She does an impressive job of acting casually interested—no eye contact, conversational tone.

"Did Izzy teach you how to get information out of people?"

"Actually, I'm pretty good at it myself." Her eyes twinkle at me from underneath her impossibly long eyelashes.

"Not as good as you think," I say, pointing at her. "Tell me about you. Did you graduate from college? What'd you major in?"

"I just graduated from UCLA. I majored in international studies and I'm headed to law school in January. At least, I'm supposed to be."

"What does that mean?"

"This whole wedding thing," she says. "I'm supposed to start at Pepperdine, but Steve wants to move back to Dallas. It got all screwy."

She stops and puts her face in her hands.

"You don't have to tell me," I say, putting my hand on her shoulder. "I'm sorry for prying,"

From the corner of my eye, I see a man rush through the door. Without even looking over, I know it's Stevie. His eyes dart around the room until they finally focus on me. He keeps it under control until he sees Elle sitting across from me with my hand on her shoulder. He charges toward me as I stand up.

"What the hell, Young?" He lunges for me, but I sidestep it easily.

"Settle down, Stevie." I catch him by the arm to prevent him from crashing into the table. As I steady him, he whips his other arm around and tries to land a punch. I block it and pin him against the wall as gently as I can.

"Nash!" Elle jumps out of her chair and runs over to us.

"I'm not going to hurt him," I say without looking back at her. "Don't try it again, Stevie."

He spins around as I release him. His eyes go from me to Elle.

"Are you okay?" He bumps me as he walks past and grabs her by both shoulders. "Babe, are you okay? Did he hurt you?"

"No, of course not." She looks over his shoulder at me. I try to soften my eyes by smiling at her.

"Did he force you to go with him?" Steve turns around and looks at me as he pushes Elle protectively behind him. I want to rip her away from him.

"No, Steve. No," she says, walking between us. She puts her hands on his chest and tries to push him back a bit. "I asked him for a ride. He was doing me a favor. I had to get out of there. He has nothing to do with this. Really. Let's sit down and talk."

She pulls him by the hand toward the table. He follows her —walking backward—not taking his eyes off me.

"Stay away from her, Young. I'm not going to tell you again." He lowers his voice a few octaves to try to save face.

As I grab my beer off the table and head over to the bar, I look at Elle one more time to see if she needs my help. She smiles up at me, but all the sparkle has left her eyes. I want to hug her so badly. I feel way too protective of her already.

"I guess he does hate you as much as you said," Gabi says as I sit down at the bar.

"He's an asshole. I can't imagine what she sees in him unless it's his family's money."

"I don't get that vibe from her at all. Maybe he's changed or she thought he'd changed and figured out he hadn't at the last minute."

"I don't know why I care anyway. I just met her."

She pats my arm as Izzy joins us. "He doesn't have the right aura for her at all if that helps, Nash. She was right to run away from him."

"Why would that help me? She can do what she wants." My voice is edgy. I try to calm it down a bit. "I mean, she seems nice. I hope she finds what makes her happy."

Izzy leans over the bar, kisses my cheek, and whispers, "I think she has, babe, although I don't think she realizes it yet, but I can tell you've already figured it out."

My eyes pop open as I look up at her. She smiles knowingly as she walks away. It seems Izzy is a mind reader.

Chapter Eighteen

NOELLE

December 22
Blitzen Bay, California

"What the hell happened? Are you telling me you ran out on your own?"

Steve sits down and shoves the condiment holder out of the center of the table. The way he's looking at me, I think he's trying to make sure nothing's in his way when he inevitably reaches out to strangle me.

"I panicked. None of it seemed right. I'm sorry. I know I didn't handle it very well."

He grunts. "Yeah, that's a huge understatement. Do you have any idea what's happening back in L.A. right now? Your mom's freaking out. My parents are threatening to sue your parents for the money they put into the wedding. The guests are walking around in circles. No one knows what to do."

"I'm sorry. I just couldn't do it. With everything that happened last night—"

"I knew that was it," he says, shaking his head. "I knew it. I told you we didn't have to move to Dallas. It was just a thought."

"You've been talking to your dad about it for two months. How could you not tell me?"

"I've had a lot of stress—finals, graduating, my playing career coming to an end. You know? It was a lot. I couldn't fight Dad, too. It was too much."

"Yeah, but we talk about stress. We talk about everything. Why didn't you tell me about it?"

"Because I knew you wouldn't want to move and then I'd be stuck in the middle of you and Dad."

"So you had him spring it on me in front of hundreds of people?"

"He didn't tell me he was doing that. He shouldn't have done that."

"So I would have found out after we got married? That's even worse."

"I was going to talk to you about it on our honeymoon—after all the stress was done. And then we'd figure it out and talk to Dad together about what we decided." He reaches across the table and grabs my hands. "We're supposed to leave for Anguilla tomorrow. Let's go there and chill for a week. We'll figure everything out."

My chest tightens and my legs start shaking. "I don't know, Steve. I don't think I can go. It doesn't feel right."

"What doesn't feel right? Anguilla or me?" He moves his

chair next to me and pulls me into a hug. My entire body trembles as I start crying.

"Babe, it's okay. We'll figure it out," he whispers. He's stroking my back, trying to settle me down, but it's making me feel worse. I pull away from him and wipe my eyes.

"I'm sorry, Steve. I need some time. I'm not sure how long. I need to be alone to think about everything."

"Okay, we'll go back to L.A. I'll bunk with Jack while you figure stuff out."

I take a deep breath. "I'm not ready to go back yet. I want to stay here for a while."

"Stay here? We're in the middle of nowhere. Why would you want to stay here?" He's starting to get angry. He points over to the bar. "Because of him? Are you kidding me? Are you having an affair with him?"

"What? No. I told you I met him today. He was my getaway car—nothing more."

"But you want to stay here with him?" He's shouting. He looks over to the bar and points. "Stay where you are, Young. I swear to God if you take one more step over here, I'll kill you."

I look over to see Nash walking toward us. His face looks deadly.

"Nash, I'm fine. Please," I say, signaling for him to stop. He looks from Steve to me. He nods at me and walks slowly backward toward the bar.

I look back at Steve. "Lower your voice. It has nothing to do with him. I want to stay here because it's a quiet place for me to be alone and think. I can't deal with L.A. right now and our families."

"If you don't come back with me right now, it's over." He leans back in his chair and crosses his arms.

"Seriously? An ultimatum?"

"You made a complete fool out of me. Do you know what people are saying about us? About me?"

"I don't care what they're saying. Who cares what people think of us? It's none of their business. It's between you and me."

He shakes his head and blows a long breath out. "You're so naive, Noelle. Stop being selfish. Not everything's about you. You need to start thinking about how your decisions affect other people."

I push my chair back a little bit. "No, I don't." My eyes start to tear up again. "I need to think about myself—what's going to make me happy. I can't make decisions based on what's going to make you happy—or my mom or your dad."

"And here I thought I made you happy." He's glaring at me. "So you're going to stay here? How long?"

"I don't know. Like the rest of this week. Maybe through Christmas. I need a little time."

He puts his hands over his face to muffle a frustrated grunt. "Christmas Eve is in two days. I'll give you until then."

"Thank you," I say. "Do you want the ring back?"

"Are we not engaged anymore?"

"I don't know. I'm not sure what's supposed to happen now?"

"I still want to marry you, despite all this," he says, standing up. "Come back with me. Everyone's still in town. We can have a party tonight and get married next week."

"I can't come back. Not right now." I take the ring off and try to hand it to him.

"Keep the ring," he says, shaking his head. "I don't even feel like I know you right now, but I'll come back up here on Christmas Eve and we can talk again. I've got your stuff in my car if you want it."

"Yeah," I say as he turns around and starts toward the door. He glances at Nash but keeps walking.

Steve grabs my bag out of his car and hands it to me. "This is all I found in your suite. Your phone's in there, too. I'll see you in a few days."

"Okay, thanks. I'm sorry, Steve. I really am."

He rolls his eyes as he gets in the car and leaves without replying. I watch his car drive up Main Street and out of sight. I feel a jacket go over my shoulders.

"You okay?" Nash's voice is soft and gentle. He wraps the jacket tightly around me.

"No, but I will be," I say, shivering. "Did you tell me you could get me a room somewhere? I'm exhausted."

"Yeah, I'll take you there." He looks down at my feet. "Elle, you're standing in the snow. Your socks are drenched. You're going to get frostbite."

I didn't even notice. I jump out of the snow and try to shake it off the socks.

"The inn's just down the street. C'mon," he says, bending down. "I'll give you a piggyback ride."

As I climb on his back, he takes off my socks and dries my feet on his shirt.

"Wait, don't take off my socks. It's so cold out here."

"Dry, cold feet are better than wet, cold feet," he says as he starts massaging them in his big, warm hands. "And I'm a little worried you don't know that already."

"Is that Ranger training?"

"That's common-sense training." He puts his arms around my thighs and takes off across the street. "And are you ever going to stop digging at my past?"

"Definitely not."

"You're a lot, Elle," he says, laughing.

I wrap my arms around his neck and lay my head on his shoulder. I'm so tired. I can barely keep my eyes open.

"It's going to be okay," he whispers as he leans his head against mine. "I promise."

Chapter Nineteen

NASH

December 22
Blitzen Bay, California

"Elle?"

In the few minutes it took me to walk to the Holly House, I swear she's fallen asleep. Her head's on my shoulder. I can feel her breath against my neck. It feels nice. I really don't want her to move.

"Yeah," she says quietly as she lifts her head.

As I put her down, her bag drops to the ground. She's just standing there, staring at me. I'm not sure she has the energy to move.

"Let's get you inside where it's warm," I say, guiding her through the door.

"You must be Noelle!" Claire strides across the room—arms outstretched.

Elle backs up into me a little bit. Just the feeling of her

leaning against me for protection sends a wave of electricity through my body. I put my arms around her tightly.

"Hey Claire," I say as she takes Elle's hesitant hands. "You said you had a room for her, right?"

"We absolutely do!" I reluctantly let go of her as Claire pulls her forward.

"And do you have some socks she can wear? Her feet got wet—"

"I have socks, slippers, a robe, a bubble bath, hot cider, and a big fluffy bed."

Elle's letting Claire pull her toward the stairs. She looks like she's sleepwalking.

I hear a phone beeping in Elle's bag. "Did Steve bring you your phone?"

She looks back at me. "Yeah, he said he did."

"Give me your number. I'll text you in the morning and we can get a coat and boots for you."

I type her number into my phone. When I look up, Claire's got her around the shoulders, leading her up the stairs to her room. Elle looks back at me.

"Get some rest," I say, smiling at her. "I'll see you in the morning."

She smiles and starts climbing again. Claire's chattering on about something. They turn left at the top of the stairs and disappear. My heart drops down to my feet.

"Claire will take care of her. You know that." Hank pats me on the shoulder.

"Yeah, I know she will."

Hank hands me a beer. "You said her fiancé was a buddy of yours?"

"Uh, I played football with him in high school."

"Got it." Hank motions me to the sitting room off the lobby. "Seems like an intense guy."

"Yeah. Did you see all that over at the bar?" I plop down in the chair by the fire. Elle's bag falls off my shoulder. "Oh, I still have her bag. I should take it up to her—"

Hank pushes me back down as I start to stand up again.

"Claire will take it to her," he says, looking at me over the top of his glasses.

"I know. I know," I say, sighing as he takes the chair across from me. "I'm getting in too deep. God, I just met her a few hours ago. I don't know why I feel so protective. Something about her . . ."

"You don't have to explain it to me." He takes a drink of his wine. "How'd my jacket work out for you?"

"Oh man, I think she's still wearing it. I need to get it back and have it dry cleaned or something."

"Nash, I don't care about the jacket. I'm trying to get your mind on something else. You want to talk about sports, cars, money?"

"Naw, man," I say, smiling, "but I appreciate the effort."

"I got you. We can talk about that kidnapping movie again if you want. I'm still not clear on it. Did they kidnap all the girls at the same time? Or like one by one?"

I stroke my beard. "Seems like it would be easier to take them all at once, right? I guess it matters how far apart they lived and stuff."

"And what weapons the men had, if any?" he says as he takes another sip of his wine.

"Right. And if they went in as a team or did individual assaults. Too many variables without watching the movie."

He nods in agreement. When Claire finally comes back down the stairs, we're deep into a conversation about my firewood.

"She wants her bag," Claire says as she picks it up. "And she's fine. She's already wrapped up in bed with a cup of hot cider."

"Do her feet have frostbite?" I look up the stairs to the last place I saw her.

"She's fine, Nash. Her feet—everything. Just give her a little space." She leans over to kiss the top of my head. "You're a sweet man."

I stand as she walks back up the stairs. I watch her disappear again. I need to get out of here and clear my head. I'll help Elle find some clothes tomorrow since I told her I would, but then I need to wash my hands of her. She's not available and the thoughts that are swirling around in my head are not going to lead me any place good.

"Nash? You want another?" Hank says, pointing to my beer.

"No, I should go. Thanks for the beer." I hand my empty to him. "I'll bring your first delivery of firewood by tomorrow."

"Sounds good," he says as he follows me to the door. "See you tomorrow, Nash."

I stand on the porch for a few minutes, looking up at the big Christmas tree. I was here twenty-four hours ago—looking at the same tree—and I didn't feel an ounce of Christmas spirit. Now, looking up at all the lights, I feel like a little kid waking up on Christmas morning.

The Runaway Bride Of Blitzen Bay

Chapter Twenty

NOELLE

December 23
Blitzen Bay, California

Do you know how badly you hurt Steve? What were you thinking? He's devastated.

I throw my phone down. It's eight in the morning. I've been in bed for almost ten hours—nine hours of near-comatose sleep and one hour of wide-awake agony. Over the last hour, I've been pouring through the hundreds of texts from friends and family that arrived as I slept. This one's from Carissa—my maid of honor—who's come down firmly on Steve's side.

Mom left me five voicemails—each of them louder and more hysterical than the one before. I stopped listening to them after number three. She sounded like she was losing her voice from screaming too much. Her voice was raspy, desperate, and disturbing. She said if I didn't call her back, she would 'kill me.'

Steve's sent me twelve texts ranging from apologetic to apocalyptic. I haven't responded to him either. I told him I needed time to think, but I guess he's not ready to give that to me. His last text came about three hours ago. It was just a line of question marks.

Kit's text is the only one that's made me feel at all supported.

Get some sleep. Take a breath. Be nice to yourself. You did the right thing. Just think about what you need, what you want. Everyone else can take care of themselves. I'll call you later. I love you.

My phone beeps again. It's Steve. I can't deal with it. I'm so tired. I cuddle farther down underneath the overstuffed duvet. My head sinks back into the mounds of silky pillows. If I'm going to be miserable, this is the place to do it. I don't think I've ever been so comfortable or warm. I'd like to disappear into this bed and never come out, but I need to get some winter clothes if I'm going to stay in Blitzen Bay for a few days.

Reluctantly, I pull back the cover. I'm still wearing the fluffy robe and socks I put on after my long shower last night. I was too exhausted to take a shower at all, but Claire convinced me I wouldn't want to wake up to my wedding hair and makeup. I look in the mirror—clean hair, no makeup. She was right.

I pull back the floor-to-ceiling, ice-blue velvet curtains on the picture window. They are the perfect frame for the wonderland I see before me. The snow's coming down harder than it was last night. The white lights outlining the chalets are twinkling through the snowflakes. I feel like I've landed in a Swiss alpine village. It's the most beautiful place I've ever seen.

A few cars are driving through town, but I can't hear anything. Either this room is incredibly well-insulated or Blitzen Bay is the quietest place on earth. My apartment in L.A. is loud all day long—beeping horns, sirens, airplanes flying overhead. I'm so used to the noise that this level of quiet seems almost abnormal. I take a long, slow breath. I think I could probably get used to it.

One of the buildings across the street has the sign—"General Store"—hanging from its eaves. It's right next to a coffee shop. I don't know what I'm going to do with the rest of my day, but winter clothes and coffee are a good start.

I throw on Izzy's clothes and the jacket Nash loaned me. The jacket still smells like him. I grab my phone again and scroll through the messages. None from him. My heart skips a beat. I feel inexplicably sad. I barely know him. I can't expect him to take care of me. It's probably for the best that he hasn't texted. I need to concentrate on my future. Now is not the time for fantasizing about a stranger, no matter how good he smells.

When I open my room door, I almost trip over a pair of boots. There's a note on them:

Good morning, Noelle! You can borrow my boots until you get your own. Use them as long as you want. I have several pairs. Let me know what else you need. Just ask!! Claire

Everyone's so nice in this town. It seriously might be the California version of *Brigadoon*—another one of Grandma's favorite movies. I wonder if Blitzen Bay is going to disappear when I leave—like Brigadoon does in the movie—and all of these lovely people right along with it. Maybe none of this is real. It seems too good to be true, especially Nash. No one is that sweet. I slap myself on the cheeks a few times to try to get him out of my head.

As soon as I walk out of the inn, I hear his voice behind me. "Elle!"

Even though it's freezing, just the sound of his voice makes a soothing warmth shoot through my body. I turn around to see him holding two coffee cups.

"Please tell me one of those is for me."

He smiles and hands me one. I take a sip and realize I'm not drinking coffee.

"This is peppermint hot chocolate," I say, looking at his blushing face.

He looks down and mumbles, "I mean, you said your grandma used to make it for you and, you know, that it was one of your favorite memories of Christmas. I thought it would maybe get you back in the holiday spirit."

I throw my arms around him and bury my face underneath his open coat. His chest feels warm and strong.

"You're the sweetest person."

He wraps his arms around me gently. "I know a long list of people who would strongly disagree with that."

"Well, they don't know you as well as I do."

"Yeah, that must be it." He laughs and takes his arms from around me. "You're shivering. We need to get you some warmer clothes."

"Wait!" I squeeze him tighter. "I'm not done hugging you yet."

He puts his arms back around me—tighter this time. "You just hug me as long as you need to."

We stand there for about a minute. I finally take a deep breath and release him.

"Thank you. I needed a hug," I say, looking up at him. "And in case you didn't know, your chest is very warm and huggable."

"Well, it's here anytime you need to hug it." He smiles and takes my hand. "Let's get you a real coat."

He pulls me toward the store. I walk slightly behind him. His wavy hair just reaches the bottom of his neck. The ends keep disappearing under his collar and then popping back up. It's just begging me to touch it. I want to run my fingers all the way through it.

He opens the store door. "You okay?"

"Yep," I say, pulling my eyes away from his curls.

"Hey, Nash." I hear as we walk into the store. I look over to see a bald man. His head and face are deeply sunburned except for a distinct outline of ski goggles.

"Hey, Jim," Nash says, shaking his hand. "You just get back from Big Bear?"

"Yeah, I've got to remember to use sunscreen next time. Who's this?" Jim says, smiling at me.

"This is my friend Elle. She needs some winter clothes."

"She definitely does. How do you come up in the mountains in the winter without warmer clothes than that?"

"Coming up here was a last-minute decision," I say, smiling up at Nash.

"Yes, very last-minute," he says, laughing. He still hasn't let go of my hand. He gives it a little squeeze.

Jim grabs a puffy coat with a furry hood off a rack. "Let's start with a coat. This is our warmest and it's completely waterproof. I'll find you some boots. What size?"

"Eight, please."

Nash helps me slip into the coat and then pulls the hood over my head. I spin around a few times to model it.

"It's perfect." He grins at me. "I'll find you a hat and gloves."

Jim returns with a pair of fur-lined boots. "I put some pants and shirts in the dressing room. Let me know if you need different sizes."

"Thanks, Jim!" I say as I half skip back to the room.

I try on a pair of fleece-lined pants and a white, fitted thermal T-shirt. When I walk out of the dressing room, Nash is settled into a big leather chair by the mirror.

"What do you think?" I look in the mirror and spin around a few more times.

"You look like you're ready to hit the slopes."

He walks behind me and pulls a hat over my head. It's robin's-egg blue.

"Wait, this is the exact color of Kit's hair!"

"Yeah, I thought it might make you feel more at home," he says, tapping the pom-pom on top of the hat.

I take a sharp breath and hug him again. "Why are you being so nice to me?"

"Because you're one of my favorite people on earth."

"What?" I say, laughing. "But we haven't even known each other for a full day."

"I'm an excellent judge of character."

"I know you're making fun of me and I don't even care," I say, nuzzling more tightly into his chest.

"Hey, I'm hungry. You want to grab breakfast at Izzy's?" He pauses, then adds. "When you're done hugging me, of course."

I laugh and release him. "I'm done and I'm starving."

"I have to take care of something before we eat," he says, grabbing his coat off the chair. "Meet me at the bar after you get all your stuff together."

"Okay, I'm buying breakfast." I point at him for emphasis. "I'm buying."

"You're not buying," he says, rolling his eyes.

"Nash—"

"We can arm wrestle for it."

"Perfect." I flex my bicep. "I'm much stronger than I look."

"Good, then breakfast will be on you." He squeezes my arm. "Yep, I've obviously already lost.

I get dressed in some of my new clothes and gather up everything else I want. I plop all my clothes on the counter and take a card out of my wallet. Jim holds up his hand.

"Put it away. This has already been paid for." He starts cutting off tags and putting everything in bags.

"What? No! Did Nash pay for it?"

"I'm sorry, ma'am," he says, laughing. "The person asked to remain anonymous. It's all going on his—*or her*—account."

I shake my head. "I'm seriously going to hurt him."

"Naw, let him spoil you. I haven't seen Nash look this happy since he moved here. I think you're good for him. Where'd you meet?" He hands me the bags.

"At a wedding," I say slowly.

"Oh yeah, that's a great place to meet someone. Unless you're the bride or groom, of course." He laughs as I turn toward the door. "See you later, Elle. Stay warm!"

Chapter Twenty-One

NASH

December 23
Blitzen Bay, California

"Jim told me someone paid for all of this. Do you have any idea who might have done that?"

Elle walks out of the store—wrapped up warmly in all her new clothes. She has the blue hat pulled down to her eyes with a long braid coming out of the side of it.

"No idea. It was probably Santa."

I grab her bags and hang them on one arm and guide her toward Izzy's with the other.

"I'm going to pay you back and I'm really annoyed with you right now." She looks up at me, shaking her head.

"Yeah, yeah. Just keep walking."

When we walk in the door, she stops so suddenly that I crash into her. I wrap my free arm around her to keep her from falling over.

"Oh my God!" she says, staring straight ahead. She leans her body back against mine.

"Are you okay?" I direct my eyes to her line of sight. She's looking at my neighbor Sam.

"It's Santa," she whispers, pressing her back further into me.

"It's not Santa. Do you think every old guy with a white beard is Santa?"

She's leaning against me like she can't be trusted to stand on her own. If I've ever met a more dramatic person, I certainly don't remember it.

"Nash, he looks exactly like Santa," she says, tilting her head up to look at me.

"Yeah, and he's wearing a red sweater. It must be him."

"Exactly!" She puts her arms on top of mine and presses them more tightly to her. "Please tell me his name is Nick."

"His name is Sam. Sorry to disappoint you."

Sam looks up from his newspaper and sees us staring. A big grin fills his face as he motions us over to his table. Elle busts out of my arms and runs over to him.

"Sorry to disturb your breakfast, Sam," I say, catching up to her. "This is my friend Elle. Elle, this is Sam."

She reaches out and holds his outstretched hand. "It's so nice to meet you."

He squeezes her hand. "It's so nice to meet you, Noelle."

She takes a quick breath. "How did you know my real name is Noelle? Are you—"

I swat her leg. "I'm sure Gabi or Izzy told him."

"It's a pretty name," Sam says, still holding her hand.

"Those of us with Christmas names are lucky. My middle name is Nicholas."

She squeals. "Oh my gosh! That's just the perfect name for you."

"Okay, we should sit down." I start bumping her away from Sam's table with my body. "Enjoy your breakfast, Sam."

"It was my pleasure to meet you, Noelle," Sam says, not taking his eyes off her. "I'm here every morning if Nash isn't available for breakfast."

"It's a date!" she says, peeking around me to get a last look at him. I continue to push her until we get to the booth in the far corner.

She slides in across from me. "Nash, his name is Nicholas!"

"His name is Sam and I'm going to need you to turn down the Christmas cheer by about a hundred percent—at least until I have more coffee."

"You live in a town named after a reindeer and your neighbor—who looks like Santa—is named Nicholas. This might be the North Pole!"

"It's not the North Pole." I laugh as I hand her a menu. "How long do you think we drove from L.A.?"

Gabi comes around the corner. "Look! She's one of us now," she says as she tugs on Elle's new coat. "You look like a native."

"Thank you!" Elle says without taking her eyes off me. "Gabi, who does Sam look like?"

"Santa Claus. Or Danny Glover. Or Danny Glover playing Santa."

"See!" Elle smiles at me and turns to Gabi.

"I have Izzy's clothes," she says, reaching for the bag she has next to her on the bench, "but I want to wash them first."

"Just give them to me. I have to throw in a load today anyway." Gabi takes the bag and throws it over to the door to her apartment.

"Oh wait, Nash, your jacket is in there, too," Elle says.

"It's actually Hank's jacket. I didn't have one, so I had to borrow it."

"That's why it was so small on you!" Elle laughs. "You looked like you were about to bust out the seams."

"What? No," I say, slowly. "Claire told me I looked good in it."

"Nash, you're like two sizes bigger than Hank and at least a couple of inches taller. Claire was trying to make you feel good," Gabi says. She turns to Elle. "I'll get the jacket back to Hank."

"Will you do me one more favor?" Elle says, trying to sneak her credit card onto Gabi's order pad. "Will you put this breakfast on there? And any other meals and/or drinks I have with Nash."

I grab the credit card before Gabi has a chance to take it. "Don't listen to her, Gabi. I'll have my usual—scrambled eggs and biscuits and gravy. If you want that, Elle, it's delicious."

She puts out her hand to get her card back—her eyebrows raise like a school teacher who's about to discipline her student.

"I will have that, Gabi," she says, still staring at me, "with a bowl of fruit, please."

Gabi looks from Elle to me, shakes her head, and walks away laughing.

"Give me my card back, Nash." She's still holding out her hand.

"Nope," I say, putting it in my wallet. "You don't get it back until you can be trusted to use it correctly."

She adjusts her arm, so her elbow is on the table. "Then we arm wrestle. Let's go."

"All right," I say, pulling my sleeve up. "I did agree to that."

I count us down and let her push my arm about halfway toward the table before I stop it. She's pushing with everything she's got. She kneels on the booth's bench and leans her entire upper body into my arm. It doesn't budge. She looks at me to see if I'm straining.

"You want to try sitting on it?" I say, shaking my head.

"I'm thinking about it."

Before she's tempted to climb on the table, I push with a little more effort. I get us back to even. She has both hands wrapped around mine, trying to resist. I push a little more until I'm leading. She looks at me, frowning.

"Are you going to stop trying to pay for breakfast?" I say as I push her hand so it's only an inch from the table.

"Never." She grimaces as I slowly push her hand all the way down. She collapses on top of our hands.

"You cheated," she says, looking up at me.

"Yes, I'm the one who was cheating there."

She sits back and crosses her arms. "Fine. You won. I'm very disappointed."

"I'm so sorry for winning. What can I do to make it up to you?"

She reaches across the table. "I'm so glad you asked. I do have something."

"Damn. You had that loaded." I look at her suspiciously. "Okay, what is it?"

"I haven't been in the snow for so long. I want to go sledding today."

"Sledding, huh? Umm, I don't have a sled," I say, stroking my beard. "Wait, I think I saw a sled on Sam's back porch."

"Who?"

"Sam," I say, pointing back at him. Her expression is blank. "Elle, you just met him—my neighbor."

"I didn't meet anyone named Sam," she says, tilting her head. She's trying the innocent look on me again. I keep telling her it doesn't work. The truth is it makes me flat out melt. I'm pretty sure she could get me to rob a bank with just that look.

"I'm not calling him by his middle name," I say, trying to look at her sternly.

"I don't want you to call him by his middle name. I want you to call him by his title—starts with an S, ends with an A."

"I'm definitely not calling him that." I'm trying hard not to smile. It's not working.

"I'll stop trying to pay for breakfast if you call him that—"

"Santa."

She smiles broadly. "What about Santa? Santa has a . . ."

I roll my eyes and sigh. "Santa has a sled."

"Yes, he does!" She reaches across the table and grabs my hands.

"Does me saying that really make you this happy?"

"Almost joyful." Her shoulders shimmy a little bit with excitement.

I shake my head. "What's the chance that you're going to turn down the cheer?"

"Hmm, let me see," she says, looking at the ceiling. "Probably about as good a chance as me winning an arm-wrestling match against you."

Chapter Twenty-Two

NOELLE

December 23
Blitzen Bay, California

"Do you need anything from your room before we go?"

Nash has agreed to take me sledding. I'm way too excited about it. Something inside me tells me it's more about spending the day with Nash than the actual sledding.

"Nope. I'm all good." I should probably get my phone, but I need a break from it.

He throws two twenties on the table and puts his hand up to stop my protest. "No! You promised to stay quiet about paying for stuff."

"I did not promise to stay quiet about anything. I'm not even sure that's possible."

"I'm beginning to realize that," he says, smiling.

He grabs my coat and holds it open for me. As he pulls it

up on my shoulders, his hands lightly touch my neck. I breathe in quickly as a chill goes all the way through my body.

"Are you still cold?" he says, putting his arm around me. "You sure you want to go sledding? You don't seem like you're built for this weather."

"I'm sure." I grab my mittens out of my pocket. "I definitely want to go."

"Wait, what happened to the ski gloves I picked out for you? Mittens are worthless."

"These match my hat." I hold the mittens up to my hat to show him.

"And if they get wet, they're worthless—"

"But I like my fingers to all be together so they can keep each other warm." He's shaking his head. "And they have snowflakes on them. See?"

"I can't argue with that logic. I don't even know where I'd start."

He puts his hand in the small of my back and pushes me toward Sam's table. Another chill shoots through my body. I shake my head to try to get the tingly feeling to go away. It doesn't help.

"Hey, Sam, did I see a sled on your back porch?" Nash says. "Elle wants to try some of the hills around here."

"Yes! I have a bunch. I haven't used them since my grandkids grew up. You're welcome to them."

"Why don't you come with us?" I say, walking around Nash and putting my hand on Sam's arm.

His eyes twinkle at me underneath his bushy eyebrows. "My dear, as much as I would love to spend my day with you,

The Runaway Bride Of Blitzen Bay

I think I'm too old for sledding. Will you let me make it up to you?"

"Of course." I sit down next to him and put my hand on top of his. "What did you have in mind?"

"My kids can't make it in for Christmas this year. Gabi and Izzy are coming to my house for Christmas dinner. Would you like to come, too?"

"Only if I get to be your date."

"It would be my honor." He looks at me and winks. His lips curl into a rosy arc in the middle of his bushy white mustache and beard. "Do you think we should invite Nash, too? So he won't feel left out."

"He can be our third wheel," I say, squeezing Sam's hand.

"It's settled then. Nash, you're in charge of making sure my date gets to me safely. Around six o'clock would be perfect. Dress is casual but festive."

"I've got you covered, Sam," Nash says as he grabs me under my arms and pulls me to my feet.

"I guess we're leaving. Bye, Sam. I'm looking forward to our date," I say, leaning down to kiss his cheek.

He beams up at me. "It will be the best night I've had in years."

As we walk out of the bar, I look up at Nash. "I love Sam so much."

He laughs. "You form attachments pretty quickly."

"He's just the sweetest old man."

"Yeah, he's a good guy. I think he's been pretty lonely since his wife died. This dinner will be good for him."

I stop in my tracks. He looks back at me as my eyes start to water.

"His wife died?"

He grabs my hand again and tries to pull me to his truck. "Yeah, it's been a few years. He's fine. Everyone's fine. There's no reason to cry."

I pull back on his hand and stare at him—scrunching up my face to try to stop the tears that are forming.

He takes a deep breath. "Are you trying to hold back your tears?"

I nod my head quickly causing a few tears to escape and roll down my cheeks.

"Will you feel better if you cry?"

"So much," I say, my voice squeaky.

He opens his arms and nods down at his chest. "C'mon then. The chest is available for crying, too."

I fall into him as the tears start rolling down. He pulls me to him and pats my back. When all the tears have left me, I take a deep breath.

"Are you done?" he says, pushing me back and leaning down to look directly into my eyes.

"For now."

After he opens the truck door, he puts his hands under my arms and lifts me to the seat. He drops his hands to my legs and smiles.

"Are you always this emotional?" he says gently.

"Only when my life's falling apart—"

"Your life's not falling apart," he says as his body rests against my knees. "It's just beginning."

I stop breathing for a second. He backs away and closes my door—his eyes stay locked with mine until he walks around the front of the truck.

As he gets in, I'm rooting through his glove compartment. "Do you have any Kleenex?"

"Uh, I don't think I do." He looks at me trying to wipe the tears off my cheeks with my oversized mittens. "Here, let me help."

He takes his gloves off and starts rubbing his fingers gently over my face. I lean closer to him. When he's done, he lets his hands linger for a second. I'm staring at him. I can't move. Why do I want him to kiss me so badly?

"Elle, are you okay? Is there something else you need to cry about?" His eyes light up as he smiles.

My brain snaps back into focus. "Not at the moment but I'm sure there will be soon. You're going to need to stock Kleenex if we're going to be hanging out."

"Noted. How long are you staying here?"

"Umm, I'm not sure. Steve's supposed to come back up here in a couple of days so we can talk again."

He jumps when I say Steve's name. "Did you talk to him last night?"

"He texted me but I didn't answer him. I need some time, you know?"

He nods his head but doesn't say anything. I can sense his mood has changed.

"How long have you lived here?" I say, trying to break the awkward silence.

"About three months."

"Did you move here after you got out of the Army?"

He turns toward me and smiles slightly. He knows I'm trying to dig for information again.

"Yeah, kind of. It wasn't planned. I stumbled across this

town when I was out exploring one day. Something about it drew me in. It felt right. Does that make sense?"

"Perfect sense. This town is magical. It's so quiet and peaceful. I could use more of that."

"Maybe you should move here." He sees my surprised face and quickly adds. "I mean you have the clothes for it now and stuff."

I sigh. "As much as I would love to spend more time here, I start law school right after the holidays. I have to get back to L.A. I'm going to spend a few more days here though. And I promise you won't have to babysit me the entire time."

He looks over at me and frowns. "You know, I think it's the law in California that when someone crawls into the back of your truck, you're responsible for that person until they leave your town."

"Wow," I say, nodding. "I didn't know that. California has weird laws."

He shrugs and smiles. "It is what it is. I don't want to be arrested."

"Fine, then you're responsible for me until I leave. I want to warn you that there will likely be more crying—maybe a lot more."

"I understand my mission, ma'am."

"Ranger talk. Hmm, I think you're starting to open up to me a little bit." I smile and tilt my head.

He points at me as he stops the truck and opens his door. "Stop looking at me like that or I will abandon you at the bottom of the hill."

I smile and turn toward where he's pointing. It's the

steepest hill I've ever seen. I hope he doesn't think we're going sledding on that.

Chapter Twenty-Three

NASH

December 23
Blitzen Bay, California

"Are you sure you don't want to go with me for this one?"

We've been sledding for about an hour—down all the hills around my house except the monster hill that goes right into the lake.

"These are one-person sleds." Her voice shakes a little bit. "I wouldn't fit on there with you."

"Well, we don't have to do this hill if you don't want to."

"I want to," she says. "I think I can do it. Just turn left after that little tree, right?"

"Yeah, or you're going to go into the lake." She's scrunching her face up, trying to concentrate. "Elle, let's just skip this one—"

"Nope!" She suddenly puts her feet on her sled and pushes off. "I've got this!"

She goes flying down the hill. I take off after her. I can tell by the way she's leaning severely backward that she's lost control of the sled. I lean into my sled to try to catch up to her. I get closer but not close enough to pull her off. She soars past the little tree. I don't think she has the strength to turn the sled. She's about thirty feet from the lake.

As I'm about to dive for her, she lets go of the front of the sled and flies backward. I jerk my sled to the side just in time to see her hit the snow hard and start rolling down the hill. I jump up and run after her. She finally comes to a stop—face down in the snow.

"Elle!" I slide into the snow next to her and roll her over.

"Oh my God!" she says through her snow-packed face. "I totally panicked!"

"Yeah," I say, wiping the snow off her cheeks. "No kidding. Are you okay?"

"I think so, but I have snow everywhere. I mean everywhere."

I pull her up slowly. "You could have hurt yourself."

I start brushing snow out of her hair. She's laughing, so she must be okay.

"That was so much fun." She shakes her body and snow falls from underneath her coat.

"You're soaked. C'mon, let's go to my house and dry you off."

She picks up her drenched mittens out of the snow. "You know I heard somewhere that dry, cold skin is better than wet, cold skin."

"You must have heard that from an Army Ranger or something. I think that's the first thing they learn in their training."

I pick up both of our sleds and push her up the hill in front of me. As she walks, snow keeps falling out of her coat. By the time we reach my back porch, she's shaking pretty hard. I guide her inside my house and help her take off her coat. More snow falls out. She shivers again.

"Damn, you really did an excellent job of getting wet." I drape my coat around her as I take off her boots. "Let's get you some dry clothes."

When we walk into my bedroom, I kick the dirty clothes on my floor to the corner. "Sorry, my house is kind of a mess right now. All the clothes in the closet are clean though. Help yourself to anything. The dryer's over there if you want to put your stuff in."

I leave quickly without looking back at her. After a few minutes, she walks out wearing one of my flannel shirts. It comes about midway down her thighs. She has a pair of my wool socks pulled up to her knees. Her face is still a little bit flush from the cold—a gentle pink glow against her ivory skin. She's taken her hair out of the braid. It's flowing wildly over her shoulders and down her back. She's the sexiest woman I have ever seen. I know I'm staring, but I can't look away.

"Do you not want me to wear this shirt?" She pulls at it a little bit exposing more of her thighs. I shake my head to try to break my stare.

"No, no. It's fine. Help yourself to anything." I look away from her and busy myself making a pot of coffee. "Hey, are you hungry? I can run into Izzy's and get us lunch."

"I'm not hungry now but I could eat a salad or something later. I'm just really tired. Do you mind if I take a nap while I'm waiting for my clothes to dry?"

When I turn around, she's sitting on the couch—her knees pulled up under my shirt and her chin resting on them. Her eyes are barely open.

"Yeah, let me grab a pillow and blanket off my bed. And I'll light a fire for you before I leave."

When I come out of the bedroom, she's curled into a little ball on the couch. I want to curl up with her and pull her to my body.

"Elle?" I whisper as I cover her with the blanket. She's already asleep. I lift her head gently and slide a pillow underneath it. She stirs for a second as she grabs the blanket and pulls it up over her face. All I can see is a few strands of blonde hair popping out.

After I get a fire going, I call into Izzy's to place our order. When I leave, Elle's still fast asleep.

As I walk into Izzy's, I see a woman with bright blue hair leaning on the bar. I didn't get a great look at Kit's face before I bailed out of the wedding, but there's no mistaking that hair.

"Oh, here's Nash. He might know where she is," Gabi says, pointing over to me.

"Kidnapper?" Kit spins around as her face lights up with a wicked grin.

"You must be Kit." I laugh as I walk over to her. "I enjoyed your rendition of "Jingle Bells" yesterday."

"Thank you. It was some of my finest work." Her eyes scan my body slowly. "You're really tall. Elle didn't mention that. And big. I like big. Your shoulders are . . . Take off your coat for a second."

"Yeah, that's not going to happen. Elle's told me enough stories about you to know that you're generally up to no good."

She leans back against the bar. "No matter how she tells the stories, every bit of trouble we got into was her idea. I was just her loyal servant."

"I don't believe that for a second," I say. "Does she know you're here?"

"I've been trying to text her all morning. I'm not getting any reply. Do you know where she is?"

"Oh yeah. I don't think she has her phone with her. We just got done sledding."

"You were sledding? How romantic," Kit says, raising her eyebrows. "What's next? Taking her ice skating on the pond?"

Gabi laughs as she walks around the bar with my two lunches. She swats my hand when I try to take them from her. "She's at your house, isn't she? I wondered why you ordered a salad."

"Yeah, I mean, she got wet in the snow—"

"Oh my God! Did you have to dry her clothes?" Kit says, looking from me to Gabi. They exchange nods. "Is she naked at your house right now, Nash?"

"No!" I take a step back from them. "I mean, she's wearing some of my clothes. Her clothes are in the dryer."

"Wow, well that's definitely the start of a porn movie," Gabi says. "Nice work. Did you push her off the sled so her clothes would get wet?"

"No! She rolled off on her own. Wait, why am I explaining

myself?" I point back and forth between them. "You two are no good for each other. Stop talking."

"He gets flustered when he talks about her," Gabi says, looking at Kit. "I noticed it yesterday."

"Hmm," Kit says, looking at me and nodding.

"I'm not flustered!" I grab the lunches out of Gabi's hands. "Kit, why don't you come back to my house? You can see for yourself that everything's completely innocent."

"Now, he's trying to add me to the mix," she says, looking at Gabi.

"Go easy on him. I'm not sure he can handle both of you." Gabi laughs as she heads back into the kitchen.

"I'm not trying to add you to the mix," I say, taking her coat and helping her into it. "There's no mix. Just innocent sledding."

"Okay, if you say so." She smiles up at me. "You're polite, too. That's another point for you."

I roll my eyes as I lead her to the truck.

"Is this the getaway vehicle?" Kit says as she jumps up on the seat.

"Yeah, she climbed under the tarp covering the bed of the truck. Do you believe that? In her huge wedding dress. She just slithered right in there."

Kit laughs. "Yeah, I believe anything. No one's ever accused Elle of being hesitant. She dives right into whatever she's doing."

"She's something else," I say, laughing.

She sighs and shakes her head. "Oh my God. You've already been bitten, haven't you?"

"Bitten?"

"By the Elle bug. Don't blame yourself. Even the strongest person could only last a few hours around her without succumbing. It's easy to fall in love with her. I did, the second she was born."

"What are you talking about?" I say, looking away from her as I back the truck out. "I barely know her."

"Denial is the first stage." She takes a deep breath. "Look, Nash, you seem like a good dude. Really. But Elle isn't as strong as she seems."

"I'm not sure I think she seems that strong—"

"She acts like she is. You know, she's like a little puppy that barks and acts all fierce because that's how a dog is supposed to act, but really it just wants to be fed and cuddled. She's sensitive and tender. And if she shows you that side, I know it's tempting to want to take care of her, but that leads to other things. With everything that's going on, maybe just back off a little bit."

"Nothing's happened and nothing's going to. I know she's in a weird place. I'm just trying to be her friend."

"I know you're telling yourself that. Be careful, not only for her but for yourself, too. She's not in the right place to start something and I would hate for you to end up as a rebound guy."

I look over at her and nod as we pull into my driveway.

Chapter Twenty-Four

NOELLE

December 23
Blitzen Bay, California

"Oh my God, Kitty! What are you doing here?"

When I wake up, Kit's crawling under the blanket with me. For a second, I thought it was Nash. I fell asleep with my face buried in his pillow. His scent transported me into a very sensual dream about him. I'm still sweating a little bit as Kit snuggles down with me and covers us up.

"Just coming to check on you," Kit says, kissing my forehead. "It seems like kidnapper is taking good care of you. Wait—"

Kit pulls back the blanket and points to my bare legs. She points at Nash. "Did you not have pants she could put on?"

"I left her in my room and told her to put on whatever she wanted from my clothes. If she's not wearing pants, that's on her."

I pull the blanket back over us. "Stop, Kitten. His pants are way too big for me. And this shirt almost comes to my knees."

"Hmm. Okay," Kit says, rolling her eyes. "I wouldn't blame you if you were trying to seduce him. He's really yummy. I mean look how big he is. You know how I like that."

"Oh my God. Please stop," Nash says as his face starts to blush. "Elle, do you want your salad?"

"I'm not hungry yet, but thank you. I'll get it later."

Kit motions Nash over to us. "You know, Nash, you can join us if you want."

"Hard pass." He picks up his lunch and grabs a beer out of the refrigerator. "In fact, I'm going to eat on the porch, so you two can have some alone time."

"Okay. Hurry back though." Kit blows him a kiss as he walks through the door. "I'll miss you!"

She sits up a bit to look at him.

"Oh my God, Elle. Why didn't you tell me how hot he is?"

"God, he's so hot, right? I thought maybe I was imagining it."

"You're not imagining it. He's just a fine, fine specimen of man." She sinks back under the blanket with me. "So, did he get wet when you were sledding? Did he have to take any clothes off?"

"Unfortunately, no."

"So, you've only seen him fully clothed?"

"He took off his sweater but he had a T-shirt on underneath. I'm not sure I can see much more without passing out. His arms are huge. I mean, seriously, I'm starting to sweat right now thinking about them."

"And, you know his chest has to be beautiful."

"Gahh. Stop," I say, burying my face in her shoulder. "The last thing I need right now is another guy to worry about."

"Who says I'm looking at him for you? You know how I love man muscles."

"Did you forget about Mateo? I thought you guys were getting serious."

"Yeah, we are." She sighs loudly. "He definitely has me all lovey feeling. I can't wait for you to meet him."

"When he answered your phone that one time, I almost fainted. His accent's so sexy."

"Right? Like I could legitimately listen to him read out of a dictionary and get hot."

I lay my head on her chest. "Maybe, I'll move to Spain and live with you guys."

"As much as I would love that, it wouldn't solve anything you're going through now." She starts stroking my hair. "Have you talked to Steve since he came up last night?"

"No, he's been texting me, but I haven't replied. I guess he's still coming up here Christmas Eve."

"Do you want him to come up here? I'm no fan of his, but if you're done, cut him loose sooner than later. There's no need to torture him."

I throw the blanket over my head and scream. "How did I get here?"

"Oh, Baby Elle," she says, sinking under the blanket with me. We used to tunnel under the blankets on Grandma's bed when she told us it was time to go to sleep. We'd stay up until all hours whispering in our blanket fort.

"You haven't called me Baby Elle since we were little kids."

She laughs. "You know, there were years when I legitimately thought you were my baby."

"You don't still?"

"No," she says, kissing my forehead. "I know it now."

"What am I going to do, Kitty?"

"You're going to go to law school and get on with your life. Then on spring break or over the summer, you're going to visit me in Spain and we're going to go to the coast and have Matty serve us fruity drinks by the sea. For now, get back to L.A. and start school."

"Do you have to go back to Spain?"

"Well, my job and my boyfriend are there, so probably." She pulls me into a hug. "Why don't you drive back to L.A. with me tonight?"

"What? And spend Christmas alone? You leave tonight."

"Yeah, I guess that wouldn't work."

"I think I'm going to stay here. There's something about this place that's helping me heal."

She puts her forehead against mine and whispers, "Yeah, that something is eating lunch on the deck right now."

"Stop. It's not him. It's just the peace and quiet. I need that for a little bit."

"For a little bit? Or forever?"

"I can't stay here forever, Kit."

"I'm glad you realize that. I was starting to wonder." She pulls the blanket back and looks out on the deck. "And Nash can't be your rebound man. You know that, right? He's too nice."

"He doesn't have to be a rebound, I mean—"

"Elle, you're a day removed from leaving a man—who you loved—at the altar. There's no way anyone—even that gorgeous man on the porch—is going to be anything other than a rebound. You know I'm right."

"Yeah, I guess. I don't want to hurt him. He's so sweet."

"I will leave you in this place on three conditions." She sits up, grabs my shoulders, and locks eyes with me. "Concentrate, Elle. I'm not leaving until you agree to these. Number one: You will stop touching Nash. No touching his arm to accentuate a point. No brushing up against him as he passes by you. No hugging and for God's sake, no kissing. Kissing turns you into a complete idiot."

"You didn't mention sex. Is that okay?"

"If you're not going to take this seriously, I will drag your butt back to L.A. right now."

"We've already hugged—innocently though. Just like friend hugging."

She puts her finger in my face. "Who do you think you're talking to, missy? There's no innocent hugging with that beautiful man. Stop it. No one could be expected to resist him once the touching begins. No more touching. Agree to it. Now."

"Fine. No more touching."

She raises her eyebrows. "Number two: I don't want you to spend Christmas alone, but you have to leave this town on December 26. It's the cutest place I've ever seen and if you stay here more than a week you will never leave, especially with Mr. Huggy being here. You leave the day after Christmas. Agreed?"

"Yeah, I need to get back and find a new place to live anyway."

"Excellent. I'm going to FaceTime you on that day and I better see L.A. in the background. I want to see smog and traffic and palm trees. Understand?"

I take a deep breath and nod again.

"And number three—and this is the most important one. When I got to the bar this afternoon, I saw a man who legitimately might be Santa Claus. You are to avoid him at all costs. You must never look at him or talk to him. He's the most adorable person I've ever seen, and I know sweet old men are like catnip for you."

"His middle name is Nicholas."

"Of course it is." She looks in the air and shakes her head. "God, you've already talked to him, haven't you?"

"He invited me to be his date on Christmas at a dinner party he's having."

"Oh God, this is much worse than I thought."

"His wife died two years ago." My eyes start to tear up again. "I can't stand him up."

"Stop! You absolutely will not stand him up." She breathes in deeply. "Go to the dinner, but don't look him directly in the eyes. I seriously think his precious face might hypnotize you. And then you'll disappear into this town and I'll never be able to find you again—like in *Brigadoon*."

I sit up straight. "I thought about *Brigadoon* this morning!"

"Of course you did. How many times do you think Grandma made us watch that with her?"

"At least a hundred. She had a huge crush on Gene Kelly."

"Huge," she says, laughing. "She always used to say he was so 'neat and tidy.' Like that was something to get hot about."

"God, I miss her. This time of year, it's brutal. What do you think she would tell me now?"

"She would tell you to get on with your life—get beyond the drama, the men with beautiful arms, the cute old Santa men—and get back to reality. Go back to L.A. and start law school. Everything else will fall into place."

I lay my head back on her chest and nod. I look at Nash out on the deck. He's leaning back with his feet up on a chair, draining the last of his beer as he looks out at the frozen lake. Kit's right. Although my body's almost physically aching for him right now, there's no way that anything that happens between us could be anything more than a rebound. And technically, I'm still engaged. Although I know it's over. I've known for longer than I care to admit.

Nash answers his phone. He jumps up and starts pacing back and forth. He glances in at us a couple of times. After he hangs up, he looks out at the lake for a minute. He looks like he's trying to figure something out. Finally, he turns around, opens the door, and peeks his head through.

"Umm, I have bad news—"

Chapter Twenty-Five

NASH

December 23
Blitzen Bay, California

"Hey. Why are you calling me? I seriously didn't even know you knew how to place a regular phone call. What's wrong?"

"Uh, we have a situation at the bar," Gabi whispers. I've never heard her lower her voice.

"What situation? Are you hurt?" My mind, as always, goes to the worst-case scenario. Military training doesn't leave you that easily.

"I'm not hurt, but I might have to kill Noelle's mom."

I jump up. "What? Elle's mom is at the bar?"

"And her dad. He seems chill, but her mom's like a raging lunatic. Iz tried to calm her down and I thought the mom was going to punch her. I haven't told her where Noelle is, but I don't think she's leaving without seeing her."

I look inside. Elle and Kit are still snuggled on the couch.

"All right. Try to keep the mom contained. We'll be there in a few minutes."

As I hang up the phone, I think quickly about going into town by myself. Elle doesn't need any more stress. I know she'd be upset if I did though. I guess I have to tell her.

I open the door and peek in. "Umm, I have bad news—"

"You've decided not to join us?" Kit lifts the blanket and pats the cushion next to her. "You can still change your mind."

"Yeah, I'm not going to join you and that's not the bad news."

"Well maybe not for you," Kit says, covering them up again.

"Gabi just called me. Elle, your parents are at the bar."

"What?" Elle sits up quickly. "What do you mean they're at the bar?"

"I mean they're at Izzy's—right now—looking for you."

"Well, that's definitely bad news." She pulls my shirt over her face and muffles a scream.

Kit stands up and tries to pull Elle up with her. Elle sinks deeper under the blanket.

"Elle, get up. Now! We have to save the townspeople before Leni terrorizes them any further."

"Ahh! I don't want to!" Elle hits the pillow before she rolls over and stands up. As she pushes herself up, I see a peek of her backside. I turn my head quickly and see Kit staring at me. My mouth's still wide open and I'm sure I have a stupid, stunned look on my face.

Kit mouths, "I'm watching you," as she shakes her head.

Elle turns around and looks back and forth between us. "What?"

"Nothing," Kit says. "I was just trying to convey to Nash how difficult Leni can be."

"That's the first time you've ever been that politically correct about it." She looks from Kit to me. "Do you think my clothes are dry?"

"Yeah, they should be," I say, heading back to the bedroom. "I heard it beep."

"Are you sure you didn't throw them out?" Kit smiles at me as I pass her.

I shake my head. "You know, you talk as much as Elle does."

"There's no need to exaggerate, Nash!" Kit yells at my back. "No one talks as much as Elle."

Elle follows me into the bedroom. "Nash, maybe you should sit this one out. It's probably going to get ugly."

"I was about to say the same thing to you," I say, putting her clothes on the bed. "Do you want Kit and me to handle this? You don't need any more stress."

"Kit hates my mom. She's just going to add fuel to the fire."

"Then I'll handle it myself. She can stay here with you." I take her shoulders and lean down to look at her. "You don't have to deal with anything you don't want to deal with right now. I've got your back."

"Thank you, but you can't protect me from this. I should have called Mom back this morning. I'm sure that's making her crazier. Believe me, she will burn this town to the ground if she doesn't get what she wants."

"I absolutely can protect you. I'm not going to let anyone come at you—even your mom."

She nods her head. She looks really tired again. I pull her to me and give her a quick squeeze.

"It's going to be fine. Get dressed. After your parents leave, if you need more hugging or crying or liquor—whatever—I've got you, okay?"

She nods again as I leave the room and close the door behind me. Kit's sitting on a kitchen stool, staring at me.

"Nash, I'm not saying this to hear myself talk. Really. I have a Ph.D. in Elle. You're wading into dangerous waters. Please back off a little bit. She's not able to think for herself right now."

I'm starting to get a little bit pissed at her. "I don't know what you think you're seeing. It's innocent. I'm just being nice to her. Nothing's going to happen."

"Oh yeah. I saw the way you looked at her butt. That wasn't a friendly look."

I shake my head as I walk over to her. "She's a beautiful woman. No man could see that and not stare for a second. Just a natural reaction. Nothing more."

I hear Elle walk out of the room behind us. She's still got my shirt on—now tied at her waist over her ski pants. "My shirt was still a little wet. Can I wear this for now?"

"Yeah, of course. Keep it," I say, walking over and grabbing their coats off the rack.

"Wait, what's wrong?" Elle says. "The mood in the room has changed."

Kit walks over and takes her coat from me. "Of course the mood has changed, Elle. Leni's energy has already enveloped the entire town."

Elle sighs and looks up at me as I help her into her coat.

"Last chance to stay out of this. Save yourself. Kit and I are used to it."

"Well, I don't know about used to it," Kit mumbles as she walks out the door.

I look down at Elle. "I'm coming with you. What did I tell you about that California law?"

"Oh right," she says, laughing as she pulls her snowflake mittens on. "But I'm telling you, you'd probably rather spend a few nights in jail than meet my mom."

Chapter Twenty-Six

NOELLE

December 23
Blitzen Bay, California

"Finally! I don't know how you ended up in this godforsaken place, but we're leaving right now!"

As we walk into Izzy's, Mom charges over to me. She grabs my arm and starts pulling me toward the door. I jerk away from her so forcefully that it causes her to trip. She's about to crash into the wall when Nash grabs her shoulders to steady her.

"Get your hands off me!" Mom recovers and slams both her hands into Nash's chest. He throws his arms in the air like someone just pulled a gun on him.

"Mom! Oh my God. Stop. This is my friend Nash," I say as I back up against him. He squeezes my shoulder to let me know he's okay.

"Your friend?" Mom takes a step toward us. I press my

body more firmly against Nash. I've seen Mom all shades of mad, but never like this. Her eyelids are blinking rapidly and she's gritting her teeth so hard that I think they might crumble in her mouth. "Steven told me about "your friend." He said you were probably having an affair with him before the wedding."

My mouth flies open. "I wasn't having an affair with him or anyone else. I met Nash yesterday. Back off. He has nothing to do with this."

Mom snorts loudly. I've never heard her do that. It makes me jump. She takes another step toward me.

"Noelle, if you don't come back with us right now and marry Steven, you are going to pay back every cent we spent on your wedding. And that includes the money that Trip Walker is threatening to sue us to recover."

Kit walks out from behind Nash. I don't think Mom has even noticed her yet.

"Oh, and of course, you're here," Mom says, swinging her arms in the air. "Any trouble Noelle has ever had in her life has started with you."

"Leni, why don't we sit down over here and get a big glass of wine?" Kit puts her hand on Mom's shoulder and tries to guide her to the corner of the room. Mom swings around and slaps Kit hard in the face.

"Oh hell no!" Kit yells as she lunges at Mom. Nash pushes me behind him and grabs Kit around the waist. He lifts her into the air as she kicks wildly and tries to break his grip.

"Stop!" he says as he carries her to the other side of the room. He puts her down and shoves her into a chair. "Stay! Don't even think about moving."

"Mom! You just hit your niece."

Mom whips around to face me. "I know she's your favorite person, Noelle, but it would be nice if you took my side just once—on anything."

Mom takes a step toward me. As I back up, I feel Nash behind me again. He puts his arm around my waist.

"Mom, Kit's not my favorite person—"

"Excuse me?" Kit yells from behind me.

"Grandma was my favorite person," I whisper. "I will never understand how you turned out so differently than her."

Mom takes a quick step back like someone punched her. For the first time in my life, I see tears coming to her eyes. She turns away.

"Leni," Dad says as he hands her the car keys. "Go wait in the car. I'll be out in a second."

She grabs the keys and charges out the door without looking back at me.

"Noelle, come over here," Dad says, pointing to a table.

Nash pulls me closer to him. "Are you okay? You don't have to do anything you don't want to."

"Who the hell are you?" Dad says.

"Dad, this is my friend Nash Young. Nash, this is my dad, Dresden Clark."

Nash extends his hand. Dad doesn't move.

"Dad, sit," I say, pointing at the table. I pat Nash's hand as I look up at him. "I'm fine. Really."

He nods at me. As he starts to walk away, he sees Kit standing up.

"Down! Sit down, crazy!" He points at Kit as he quickly

closes the distance between them. "You're not following her outside."

"I was trying to get a drink, bossy. Do you think that would be possible?"

"I'll get it for you. Sit! Don't make me chase you, Kit," he says, walking backward to the bar—his eyes fixed firmly on her.

"Who is that guy? Is there something you want to tell me?" Dad says.

"He's just a friend. Nothing to tell." I sit down across from him. "Dad, I'm sorry. I'll pay you back for everything if it takes me the rest of my life."

He reaches over and holds my hand. "You don't have to pay us back for anything. Your mom's just venting."

"Why is she like that?"

He sits back and sighs. "She wasn't always. When I met her, she was wild and carefree—just like you."

"That can't be true," I say, taking a sip of the drink Nash just dropped off for me. "What happened to her?"

Dad shakes his head, looking down. "I happened to her, Noelle. I haven't been the best husband."

"What?" My eyes start to tear up. "Did you cheat on her?"

"No, nothing like that. I've just never been there for her, not like I should have been."

"What are you talking about? You were always there for us."

"For you. I was always there for you, but not for her. The second we got married, I abandoned her for work. I spent most of my time at the office and when I was home, I wasn't really.

I left her to fend for herself. I don't know why it's taken me so long to realize that."

"You're a great dad."

"I hope so, but I haven't been a great husband. I always made her play bad cop with you." He smiles and nods toward Kit. "You know you and blue hair over there were kind of holy terrors growing up. I ignored it and made your mom deal with it. I should have been there for her. I should have backed her up."

"It's not too late."

"I hope not," he says, leaning back in his chair. "I'm going to try—starting now. You don't have to pay us back for any of the wedding stuff, but you have to start paying your way. I'll put a little money in your account to get you started, but if you're going to stay in L.A., you need to figure out a way to make it work. You're an adult now."

I nod. "That's more than fair. I can grab more hours at work. I'll be fine."

"Work? What work?"

"I work at a restaurant near campus. I'm a waitress."

"You work?"

"Dad, I've worked since freshman year. I've been saving for law school. I'm still going to have to get some student loans and stuff, but I'll be okay."

He shakes his head. "You know, I'm not sure how I thought you were paying for law school. I guess I thought you had a scholarship like UCLA."

"Nope. I'm paying for this one, but I'm good. I'll be fine."

"How are you going to pay rent though? You and Steve have the lease until the end of January, but if he's not living with you, you'll have to find a cheaper place. Have you talked to him? Is it over for real?"

"We talked last night and he's supposed to come up again, but I think it's over, Dad."

He nods his head slowly and sighs. "I'm sorry, honey. I know it can't be easy."

"Thanks, Dad. I'll be okay."

"Are you sure you want to stay in L.A. by yourself?" He narrows his eyes. "I'll worry about you being there alone."

"I'll be fine. All I know right now is that I want to start law school in a few weeks."

He takes a deep breath. "Then you're going to have to find a cheaper place to live."

"I've got it. I'll get a little studio or something. I'll be fine."

"Okay, but if you're struggling, call me. I don't want you starving or anything."

"I'm not going to starve, Dad. I promise." I smile and pat him on the hand. "You better get outside before Mom drives off and leaves you here."

He laughs as he stands up and hugs me. "She probably already has. I love you, Noelle, and so does your mom."

"I know, Dad. I love you guys, too. I'll call you when I get everything set."

He nods. "Do me a favor, okay?"

"Anything."

"Find a guy who puts you first—above everything. Someone who will always have your back."

I nod as he hugs me again. He looks over to Kit.

"See 'ya, Kit," he says, smiling. "Safe travels back to Spain. Sorry about the slap."

"It's all good, Uncle Dres." She runs over and hugs him.

As I watch him walk out the door, Kit puts her arm around my shoulder. "Babe, I've got to go, too or I'm going to miss my flight. Walk me outside."

"Okay, but you better give Nash a hug before you leave," I say, laughing through the tears that are starting to form.

"Hell no. I'm not touching him either." She waves to Nash. "Bye, kidnapper. Thanks for rescuing Elle."

"Bye, Kit," he says, smiling. "It's been interesting."

"Of course it has," she says, pulling me out the door. She gives me one last hug. "I'll see you in March. And we'll talk every single day until then. Okay?"

I nod at her as she wipes the tears off my cheeks.

"Grandma would be so proud of you."

"You think?" I say quietly.

"I know. You saw what she had with Grandpa. She wouldn't want her precious Elle to have anything less than that."

"You're right."

"I know I am," she says as she gets in her car. "I love you, Baby Elle. I'll call you from the airport tomorrow."

"Love you, Kitten! Merry Christmas!"

I wave until her car drives out of sight and then collapse on the bench in front of Izzy's.

Chapter Twenty-Seven

NASH

December 23
Blitzen Bay, California

"You decided not to leave, huh?"

Elle turns to me and smiles. "Yeah, I'm not sure why I would leave the North Pole right before Christmas, especially when I have a date with Santa Claus coming up."

"I'd almost forgotten about that. You definitely can't stand up Santa."

"Thank you for finally admitting who he really is," she says, laughing.

"Well, we don't like to reveal his true identity to strangers until we know they're true believers."

"I completely understand."

"Do you want company?" I say, walking over to her.

"If you even want to be seen with me after all that."

"It wasn't that bad and you gave Izzy something to talk about for months."

I sit down next to her and put my arm around her. She jumps a little bit and leans away from me. I push my arm quickly onto the back of the bench—not touching her. Something has changed. I'm guessing Kit gave her the same warning she gave me.

"Kit told me this afternoon you might go back to L.A. with her tonight," I say, looking away from her.

"She wanted me to. I probably should have."

"I thought you said you wanted to hang out here a little bit and unwind."

"I do, but she knows me better than anyone."

"No, she doesn't," I say as I lean my head back against the wall. "You know you better than anyone."

She looks at me and frowns. "She always knows what's best for me."

"There's no doubt she wants what's best for you, but you're the only one who knows what that is. You can listen to everyone's advice—hers, mine, your parents—but you're the only one who should be deciding what's best for you."

"I don't think I can do that right now. My mind's too muddled. I need someone to tell me what to do."

"No, you don't. And you don't have to decide what to do right now. Just sit with it. Give it time to come to you. If you rush it, you're going to make the wrong decision. Just breathe and give yourself a break. And definitely stay away from your mom for a while."

She covers her face with her hands and groans. "Why is my mom so crazy?"

"Everyone has a little crazy in their family," I say, laughing. "Nothing wrong with it."

"You've only told me a little about your mom, but she sounds lovely, not crazy."

"Maybe it skips a generation. My mom's cool, but my grandma was a little, uh, unusual."

"Prove it." I see a little life coming back to her eyes. "I don't think you have any 'unusual' in your family."

"Okay," I say, sitting up, "you asked for it. Let me see. Umm. So my grandparents lived on a little farm in the middle of Texas. When they retired, they got a bunch of chickens to keep them entertained. My grandma made them outfits."

"Wait. What do you mean outfits?" She starts to smile.

"Shirts and matching hats."

"Hats? What? Oh my God. What kind of hats? Like bonnets? Or cowboy hats? Or like little party hats? I have to see them. Please tell me you have pictures." She puts her hand on my leg.

"I'm sure my mom does somewhere."

"This is amazing. Did the chickens like the outfits?"

"No, no, they definitely did not. They pecked them off each other's bodies. One of the hens got some of the material caught in its throat."

"What?" She squeezes my leg. "Did he die?"

"First, hens are female, but yes, she did die. Grandma had a funeral for her."

She puts her hand over her eyes and shakes her head.

"Elle, are you crying again? It was just a chicken."

She peeks at me through her fingers. "I'm a very sensitive person, Nash. If we're going to be friends, you're going to have to embrace my crying. And I thought you said she was a hen, not a chicken."

"They're all chickens. Hens are female; roosters are male, but they're all chickens."

"That's unnecessarily confusing." She throws her hands down.

I smile. "Well, I will call the chicken board tomorrow and file an official complaint."

"Is there really a chicken board?"

"There's not a chicken board, Elle. How are you this gullible?"

"Are you sure there's not? I mean someone has to be regulating them, right?"

"Why is this important to you?" She's looking at me very intensely. "I mean, there might be a chicken board—like in Arkansas or something."

"Do you want to research it a little bit more and get back to me?"

I shake my head. "You're getting me off my original point."

"There was a point to this?" she says, smiling and tilting her head.

"Yes, there was," I laugh. "My point was: don't worry about your mom because everyone has stories to tell about their families."

She sits up straighter. "Yeah, but your grandma was adorable crazy. My mom's scary crazy."

"People react differently to stress. Your mom just doesn't handle it well."

"Understatement—"

"Honestly, she can't be that crazy because she raised you and you're . . . you're pretty perfect."

I reach out and take her hand. She breathes in quickly and bites her lip. Her eyes get wider as she looks from our hands up to my eyes.

"Look, Elle, I know you're not in any place to start something, but I need to be honest with you. If you were available, I would be all over you."

She laughs. "All over me, huh?"

"Respectfully, of course," I say, smiling. "You are attractive to me in every single way possible."

She takes a deep breath. "I think you're amazing, too, and I'm wildly attracted to you—"

"Wildly? Okay, that's a good start." I say, laughing as I brush her cheek with my hand. She pulls back a little bit. "I know you're not available. It's fine. I just wanted you to know the truth. And that's all it has to be right now."

She scoots over to me and then lays her head on my shoulder. I put my arm back around her and pull her closer to me.

"Are you thinking for yourself now?" I whisper into her hair.

"Yeah," she says, "but honestly, I don't think I know what I'm thinking and I definitely don't know what I'm doing."

"Just breathe. There's no rush about anything."

She nods her head against my chest. We sit like that for a minute before I pull her up.

"I want to show you something." I take her hand and start leading her down the street.

She pulls back a little bit. "What do you want to show me?"

"Would you just come on and quit questioning everything?"

I put my arm around her and pull her to the big Christmas tree by the Holly House.

"When I came into town to get our lunches earlier, I brought a load of firewood for Hank. I was unloading it and lost control of an armful. One of the logs rolled under the tree. When I climbed under to get it, I saw something. C'mon, I want to show you."

I get down on my knees and start to crawl under the tree. She's still standing. I pull her hand until she's kneeling by me.

"Trust me. You'll like this."

"Fine," she says as she starts to crawl under the tree with me.

We get to the center of the tree. "Okay, close your eyes and rollover."

"Excuse me!" She looks at me with her eyebrows raised almost to her hairline.

"Not like that. Just do it."

She lets out a dramatic sigh, but closes her eyes and rolls over on her back. I lie down next to her.

"Okay, open your eyes."

"Ohh!" She takes a breath in as she looks up at the fifty feet of twinkling white lights above us. "Nash, it's so beautiful."

"Yeah, it is," I say, turning my head to look at her. "I thought of you when I saw it."

She scoots closer to me and wraps her arm around mine. We lie there for a few minutes watching the lights twinkle above us. She suddenly pops up on her elbow and looks at me.

"Wait, did your grandma bury the chicken in one of the little outfits?" Her brow's furrowed like she's been thinking about this for a while.

I smile. "You know, I've never thought of that, but yeah, she probably did."

She lays her head on my chest. "I love your grandma."

"I know you do." I wrap my arm around her and rest my head against hers. Her hair smells like the magnolia tree in my mom's backyard. "And believe me, Grandma would have loved every bit of you."

Chapter Twenty-Eight

NOELLE

December 24
Blitzen Bay, California

"Elle, Nash is here to see you."

Claire knocks on the door. I've been awake for about fifteen minutes, but I'm still in bed. I can't quit thinking about how Nash looked at me when he left last night. He walked me to the front door of the inn and hugged me. When I let go, he only released me an inch or so. His arms were still around my shoulders and he was looking down at me. His eyes were gentle and hungry at the same time.

I froze. I didn't know what to do or say. I wanted to take him up to my room so badly and that feeling scared me to death. I think he sensed I wasn't ready. He kissed my forehead, smiled, and walked back to his truck. I watched him until he drove out of sight and still stood there another ten minutes. I couldn't move.

"Are you up yet? Do you want me to tell him to go away?"

I roll over to look at my phone. It's almost ten. I haven't slept this late in a long time. I have a text from Nash from just before eight.

Hey. Where are you? I have to run into Big Bear. Do you want to come with me?

"Good morning, Claire," I say, sitting up. "It's fine. He can come up here if he wants."

"Okay. Are you hungry? I'm shutting down the buffet. I'll send some breakfast and coffee up with him."

"That would be great. Thank you!"

I jump out of bed, unlock the door, and dive back under the covers. I'm not ready to get up yet. I pull the blankets around me tighter.

"Hey," Nash says as he knocks lightly on the door. "Claire sent up some breakfast. Okay if I come in?"

"Yeah, it's unlocked."

He opens the door a crack and looks in. "How are you still in bed? It's almost ten."

"That's judgment I don't need right now." I pull the duvet over my head. "You can turn right back around."

"Are you going to stay in bed all day? Let me rephrase that. You're not going to stay in bed all day."

I flip the duvet off my face. "Are you looking at this bed? It's made for staying in all day."

My phone beeps. I pull the cover back over my head.

I hear him pick up my phone. "It's from Steve. Has he been texting you all night?"

"Yeah. I haven't texted him back."

"And you don't have to, but you do have to get out of bed and at least eat something. Are you hungry?"

"I'm starving."

"Okay, princess. May I serve you breakfast in bed?"

I peek out. I'm guessing Claire made him leave his coat and boots at the door because he's just wearing jeans, a white T-shirt, and socks. His hair's messy like he just pulled off a hat. He looks so sexy.

"Hello? Elle? Do you want breakfast?"

"Oh, yeah," I say, sitting up. "Thanks."

He pats the duvet. "Are your legs under there somewhere? This is the most insanely thick blanket I've ever seen."

"It's amazing. I have never been this warm," I say as I take the tray from him. "This is a lot of food. Do you want some?"

"I already ate breakfast—when it was still morning," he says, raising his eyebrows, "but yeah, I can always eat more."

I pat the bed and motion for him to sit next to me. He hesitates.

"What? Are we in Victorian England? You can sit next to me in bed without me losing my virtue."

He smiles as he scoots over next to me. "Yeah, especially in this bed. I don't think I could find you under all these covers even if I tried—"

"Hmm. I was hoping a Ranger would have better search skills than that."

"You were hoping that, huh?" He smiles down at me.

"Maybe, but apparently you're not willing to put in the work."

"I definitely didn't say that. Just give me the signal and I will start searching immediately. I mean, now that I know you're wildly attracted to me and all."

His eyes are sparkling mischievously at me. I change the subject.

"Are you just going to eat bacon?" I slap his hand as he reaches for another piece. "You know there's fruit on the tray, too. Maybe a banana to go with all that grease."

"That's judgment I don't need right now," he says, nudging me with his shoulder. "And don't think I didn't notice you changing the subject, Miss Open Book."

"I'm sorry, Nash," I say. "I'm not ready."

"I know you're not and you don't have to ever apologize to me," he says as he takes another piece of bacon off the tray. "Kit told me to back off. I should probably take her advice. Honestly, I'm a little scared of her."

"That's very wise. She doesn't mess around where I'm concerned. Although, she told me to stay away from you, too. I think she kind of likes you. She said she doesn't want you to be my rebound guy."

He laughs. "I don't want to be a rebound guy. Does it have to be like that?"

"I think that's all it can be right now. I mean, I'm still technically engaged."

"Only technically?" He locks his eyes with mine. "He's coming up today, right?"

"He's supposed to be. I haven't talked to him."

"Do you want him to come up here?"

"I don't care either way. Does that sound horrible? I have to break up with him and I'm being a wimp about it."

"No, it doesn't sound horrible, but yeah, you should probably do it sooner than later. He needs to move on with his life, too."

"You're right. Everything's so crazy right now. It makes me want to stay in this bed and never come out."

"Well, we definitely can't have that," he says, standing up. "I came to get you. I have to run some stuff over to Big Bear. Why don't you come with me?"

"What stuff?"

"Just some stuff Sam and I made that we sell over there. C'mon, get up."

He tries to pull the duvet off me. I tug it back from him and sink back into my pillows.

"I might go with you if you tell me what we're delivering."

"Quit being so nosy. And there's no 'might' about it. You're going if I have to pull you out of this bed." He grabs the duvet again. "Elle, are you going to make me pull you out?"

I sigh and roll my eyes. "I will go, but only because you're making me."

I whip the duvet back. I realize too late that the T-shirt I'm wearing only comes to my waist. He takes a slow scan of my bare legs from my feet all the way up. His eyes stop when they reach my undies. He's not moving.

"Nash?" I say, pulling the duvet back over me quickly.

"Yep, yep. I'm fine," he says as he turns around. "Why don't I let you get dressed? I'll be downstairs."

After he closes the door, I hear him yell, "I'll come back up here if you're not in the lobby in ten minutes."

"Stop being so bossy!" I yell at the closed door. "You're no longer one of my favorite people."

I throw on a pair of jeans and a white tank top covered by a gray v-neck sweater. I pull my hair over into a messy side braid, brush my teeth, splash some water on my face, and I'm out the door. As I make it to the top of the staircase, Nash is looking up.

"Ten minutes and thirty-two seconds," he says, pointing to his phone.

"I'm always five minutes late everywhere I go, so if you go by that logic, I'm four minutes and twenty-eight seconds early."

"That's not logic. That's tardiness and it's unacceptable," he says, pulling me over to the bench by the front door. He grabs my boots and starts putting one of them on me.

"You know, I can put on my boots," I say, reaching for the other one. He swats my hand away.

"This is a full-service excursion."

"Maybe you should start offering this to all the tourists. You could make a lot of money."

He finishes and stands up—pulling me up with him. He holds my coat open for me.

"I only accept clients who crawl into the back of my truck. Luckily that limits my responsibility only to crazy runaway brides."

"On behalf of runaway brides everywhere, we accept your proposal."

He zips my coat and leans closer to me. "The other runaways can tie their own shoes. I think I've made it pretty clear that you're the only one I'm interested in."

The Runaway Bride Of Blitzen Bay

Chapter Twenty-Nine

NASH

December 24
Big Bear, California

"Why won't you let me see what's in the bag?"

Elle's figured out that the blocks I'm delivering are in a bag behind my seat. She's kneeling on the truck bench, trying to get inside it. I push her back with my free arm, trying to make a turn in the road with my other arm. I take it a little too sharply and she falls against me. My arm wraps around her—pressing her to my chest—so she won't hit her head on the steering wheel.

"Would you stop?" I gently move her back to her side. "And put your seat belt on before you go through the windshield."

"Is it meth?" She's staring at me—arms crossed with pouty lips.

"Yes, Elle. Sam and I are manufacturing and selling meth."

I roll my eyes. "You're not going to stop, are you?"

"I think we both know the answer to that."

I sigh, reaching my arm over the seat to grab one of the gift boxes in the bag. She opens it, revealing a set of brightly painted blocks.

"These are toy blocks."

"I know what they are."

"But wait, you said it was something you and Sam make. Do you make these?"

"Yeah."

"Like by hand?"

"Just like that. I carve them and Sam paints them."

"Nash, these are beautiful. And you sell them at the resorts?"

I shrug. "Yeah, Sam does. He gives the profits to the hospice center that cared for his wife right before she died of cancer."

She takes a quick breath. When I look over, she's holding her breath and her eyes are brimming.

"His wife died of cancer?" she says, exhaling slowly.

I grab her hand. I'm trying to prevent her from crying. You think I would have learned by now that it's not possible. Her eyes are so full that I'm not sure how she can see.

"Elle, you already knew she died."

"But there's new information." She protests. "You hand carve toy blocks and then give them to your adorable old-man neighbor who paints them, sells them, and then donates all the profits to the people who took care of his dying wife. That's a lot."

"You're right. It warrants another cry," I say, squeezing her hand as I watch the tears flow down her face. I reach over and pop open the glove compartment—now stuffed with those little personal packs of tissues.

"You got me Kleenex," she says, sniffing.

"I figured we would need them." I give her hand another squeeze as we drive into the resort. "Do you want to come in with me?"

"Yes," she says, turning the rearview mirror toward her to wipe the remaining tears away. "Do I look like I was crying?"

"You look beautiful—like you always do," I say as I open my door. "Slide out this way. There's a snowdrift on your side."

She slides across the seat and sits on the edge for a second. She looks up at me. This would be the perfect time to kiss her. I came close last night, but her eyes told me she wasn't there yet. She's looking at me with that same expression now. I've wanted to kiss her since her head popped out from underneath my truck's tarp on her wedding day. I know I have to be patient, but it's getting almost impossible. I smile as she takes my hands and hops down out of the truck.

When we walk in the front door, she stops suddenly, causing me to crash into her again. For a second, I think she sees another Santa Claus until I look at her face. She definitely doesn't look happy. I look across the room and see why. Trip Walker is about thirty feet from us with his tongue shoved down the throat of a voluptuous, young redhead.

"Holy crap," Elle says, spinning around so she's facing me. She tries to push through me toward the door. Too late.

"Well, well, well, look what we have here." Mr. Walker

walks over to us slowly. "I'm not sure why I'm even surprised. Nash, you've taken things away from Steve since you were boys—girls, awards, scholarships. I guess his fiancé shouldn't be any different."

"It's not what it looks like—"

He puts his hand up to stop me. "Nope. I don't even want to hear it. I can't wait to tell Bitzy. She's been wondering how to explain it to our friends. This will make it easier for her. I can't say it's going to make it easier for your mom though."

I try to take a step toward him, but Elle spins around to face him—pressing her back against me. "And I can't wait to tell your wife about that redhead whose face you were just inhaling."

Mr. Walker laughs. "Oh, Noelle. Do you think anyone is going to believe anything you say at this point?"

"Nope, so good thing I got a picture. And I also have a picture of you and the tall brunette at Nobu a couple of months ago," she says, taking a step toward him. I pull her back. "Steve was with me that time. Yeah, that's right. Your son knows you're whoring around L.A. Does Bitzy know? I'm guessing not. How about all your friends at church? And, let me see, you've been married more than forty years—back when you were still poor—so I'm guessing Bitzy didn't sign a prenup. I wonder if she can claim California residency since you just bought that place in Malibu, then she could get half of everything."

He takes a step closer to her and grabs her shoulder. "You really are a little bitch."

"Hey! Watch your mouth." I push him back and pull her

behind me. "You ever touch her again, you will lose that hand. You understand me?"

He looks over his shoulder quickly to see if any of his group is watching. They aren't. He puts his hands up in surrender.

"I have no desire to be near either one of you ever again," he says, looking around me at Elle. "How about we call it even?"

Elle tries to walk around me. I block her with my arm. "Leave Nash and his mom alone. They've got nothing to do with this. And while you're at it, back off my parents. And tell your wife to do the same."

"We will back off everyone on one condition." He points his finger at Elle. I want to knock it down, but I resist. "If you ever see me again, you act like you don't know me. Both of you."

"Gladly," Elle says loudly. "I wish I didn't know you."

He smiles and backs away. "Nash, if you ever get her to the altar, watch out. She's a slippery one."

I wait until he's back with his group and then turn to Elle. I half expect her eyes to be filled with tears, but they're cold and hard. "You okay? You don't look like you want to cry."

"I don't cry when I'm mad," she says. "I want to kick his butt."

I smile as I put my arm around her and turn her away from him. "Okay, but before the butt-kicking begins, maybe we should get lunch. I barely let you finish your breakfast. You'll need some more energy."

"Yeah, I probably need more protein if I'm going to fight him, right?"

"That's the second thing they teach us in Ranger school—load up on protein before you kick someone's butt," I say, pulling her harder in the direction of the restaurant.

"I could probably teach Ranger school at this point." She finally turns around and starts walking with me.

"There's no doubt in my mind," I say, smiling down at her.

Chapter Thirty

NOELLE

December 24
Blitzen Bay, California

"If you don't tell me what room she's in, I'll beat on every door until I find her!"

I jolt awake and look around quickly. I'm in my bed at the Holly House. I swear I just heard Steve's voice, but it must have been in a dream. I shake my head and look at my phone. It's almost eleven. Nash dropped me off after we got back from Big Bear around five. I was so worn out from our run-in with Trip that I went right to bed. That must be why I'm dreaming about Steve.

"Man, back off! I'm sick of this stupid town. Are you going to tell me where she is or do I start breaking down doors?"

That was Steve's voice and I'm not asleep. I throw on a pair of leggings and Nash's flannel shirt. When I get to the landing, I see Hank blocking Steve from the stairs. Claire's running around in circles behind them.

"Steve! What are you doing here?"

He looks up and glares at me. The hatred in his eyes makes me freeze halfway down the stairs.

"Oh, look, there she is, my slutty fiancé."

He takes a step back and waves his arms up at me.

"Why don't you go back to your room, Noelle?" Hank says without looking back at me.

Claire looks like she's about to start crying.

"No, it's fine. You guys can go back to bed. Steve and I need to talk."

Hank's still blocking the stairs. When I pat him on the shoulder, he hesitantly moves his arm to let me by.

"Is he up in your room right now?" Steve grabs my arm as he nods up the stairs.

"No one's in my room," I say as I yank my arm away from him. "And if you touch me again, this is going to end badly for you. If you want to talk, we can go outside."

"He's not coming with us." Steve nods toward Hank who's standing right behind me.

I turn to Hank. "I'm fine. Thank you. I'm sorry for the disturbance. It's all good. You can go back to bed."

"I'm not going to bed until you're back in your room," Hank says. "Go outside if you want, but I'm watching you. I don't trust him."

Steve takes a step toward Hank, but I push him back. "Let's go, Steve. Your problem is with me, not him."

I throw on my coat and follow Steve out to the porch. He whips around as soon as the door closes.

"So you weren't having an affair with Nash, huh? Dad told me he saw you with him today."

"We're not having an affair," I say as I walk over and sit on the bench. "I met him on our wedding day. Believe what you want, but that's the truth."

"How am I supposed to believe that, Noelle? You're running around with him. Dad said he was all over you."

"I'm not having an affair with him. We're friends, but does it matter? This isn't about him. It's about you and me."

He slams his fist down on the hood of his Jeep. "You and me? Seems like it's just about you. You're doing what you want. Maybe I should sleep with a few people to even us up a bit."

"We're done, Steve," I say, standing up. "I'm sorry I left you at the altar. I'm sorry I didn't break up with you months ago when I knew it was over. I'm sorry I hurt you. I'm sorry I handled this badly, but it's done. You think whatever you need to think to help it make sense to you."

"You're such a bitch." He falls back against the Jeep like his legs won't hold him up anymore. "I can't believe you're doing this. You're so selfish. I never realized that about you until now."

"I will apologize for a lot of things I did wrong, but I'm not going to apologize for doing what's best for me. I thought that was you, but it's so obviously not. You're not the person I thought you were."

"Yeah, neither are you." He laughs bitterly. "You know, I'm glad it's over. It saves me from having to divorce you a year from now when I figure out what a little whore you are."

I walk toward the door. "I'm going upstairs to get your ring and then I want you to leave."

He makes a grunting sound. I don't look back. Hank's leaning on the wall, looking out the window. Claire's sitting at the front desk.

"I'm so sorry about this," I say, looking at them as I run up the stairs. "He'll be gone in a minute. I just need to get something for him."

When I get back outside, Steve's sitting on the bench. I walk over and hand him the ring.

"When did you take it off?" He takes the ring as he slumps over—his elbows resting on his legs with his face in his hands.

"The first night I got here after you left the bar—"

"So you've known for that long?"

I sit down by him. "I've known for a while, Steve. I just couldn't admit it to myself. I thought for a few years that you were one person, but for the last few months, you've been someone else. And tonight, you proved you're not the person I thought you were at all. I wouldn't be happy in this marriage and frankly neither would you. Now unless you can think of any more names to call me, you need to leave."

He stands up abruptly and walks toward his Jeep. He stops when he gets to the door and turns around.

"If Dad hadn't mentioned the move to Dallas, would we be married right now?"

"I don't know. I guess it's a good thing for both of us that he said it."

He stares at me. He doesn't look mad anymore. He looks tired.

"I'm not sure I agree with that," he says. "Not yet, but I probably will one day."

He shakes his head as he gets in the car. He sits there for a few minutes—looking at me.

When he finally backs out and drives away, I see Nash's truck across the street. He waits for Steve to leave and opens his door.

Chapter Thirty-One

NASH

December 24
Blitzen Bay, California

"Hank called me. Are you okay?"

When I walk across the street, Elle's staring straight ahead. Her eyes aren't blinking.

"Elle?" I say as I put my hand on her shoulder. "Did he hurt you? Hank said he was pretty upset."

She shakes her head and looks at me. "No, he didn't hurt me. Well, maybe verbally, but his screaming was kind of cathartic. I feel like I deserved a little bit of that."

"You didn't deserve that—"

"Yeah, I did." She looks up at me. "Hank shouldn't have called you. I'm fine."

"Okay," I say, nodding, "but I came all this way, you mind if I sit here with you for a second?"

"Yeah, that thirty-second drive must have been exhausting." She laughs. Her eyes light up a little bit.

"Sitting in my truck while you two finished your talk was the exhausting part. Do you know how hard I had to fight coming over here and throwing him into next Tuesday?"

She smiles and pats my leg. "I'm very proud of your restraint. By the way, if you're wondering, Trip told him about seeing us at Big Bear."

"I figured. He's an asshole. Both of them are. Sorry if that offends you."

"It doesn't." She lets out a long sigh. "Remember a few nights back when you asked me if I was going to give Steve another chance and I didn't answer you."

"Yep." I try to play it off casually, but it's all I've been thinking about since I asked it.

"Well, I didn't answer you because I was still processing everything that was happening, but the answer is no. I'm not giving him another chance. I gave him back the ring. We're done."

I take a second to let that sink in. "Are you done because you want it to be done? Or because he's pissed off?"

"I've wanted it to be done for a long time. I finally got up the nerve to end it. I don't want to spend another second with him, much less the rest of my life."

"I'm sorry you've had to go through all of this," I say, putting my arm around her, "but I'm glad you're doing what's right for you."

She looks up at me and nods. "Can we talk about something else? Anything else."

"Okay," I say, looking at her feet, "how about we start with you explaining to me why you're just wearing socks again. You do realize it's winter, right? Look there's snow right there. Do you remember those things we bought you yesterday? I think they're called boots."

She rolls her eyes. "I didn't have time to put them on when Steve got here. He was making a scene. I just wanted to get him outside. I thought poor Claire was going to start crying."

"Hmm, let's go inside." I pull her up and guide her back through the door.

Hank's at the front desk. "Everything good?" he says, smiling when he sees me.

"Yeah, he's gone." I nod toward the sitting room. "We're going to sit in here for a second if you don't mind."

"It's all good. I'm going to bed. Nash, will you snuff out the fire before you leave?"

"I've got you." I nod to him as he heads to the back of the inn.

Elle's curled up on the couch right in front of the fire. I grab a blanket off the ottoman and cover her feet with it as I sit down.

She smiles. "You know for someone I've only known for two days, you take really good care of me."

"Someone has to or you'd be running all over the place with no shoes, jumping into the backs of stranger's trucks, trying to fight people with insufficient protein supplies."

"Well, thank God, I have you looking out for me." She's smiling at me—her eyes sparkling. "So, I answered the question about Steve. I get to ask you another one."

I shake my head and laugh. "I think we're about even right now."

"Nope. Not even close. You definitely owe me one."

"All right," I say, sighing. "Let me have the question, but I reserve the right not to answer, as always."

She sits up straighter. "Why did you retire from the Army?"

I take a deep breath and sit back. My face must reflect what I'm suddenly feeling inside because her eyes get very serious. She crawls across the couch until she's sitting next to me.

"Nash, you don't have to answer. I'm sorry."

I take another breath and wrap my arm around her. She puts her head on my shoulder.

"No, it's fine. I don't talk about it a lot. I got injured on a mission. Some shrapnel in my knee. It messed up my kneecap pretty badly. There's no way I could stay on the team I was on. I couldn't move as fast as I needed to anymore."

She takes my hand and starts massaging it. "I'm sorry. I can't imagine how hard that was."

I nod my head, burying my face in her hair. I have a sudden urge to tell her about Mikey—about how he died on that same mission. She's nuzzling into my shoulder. I want to tell her so badly, but I stop myself.

"So what do you want to do now that you're retired?"

"I'm not sure, to tell you the truth." I start running my hand up and down her arm. "Gabi and Izzy want me to buy into the bar. They need someone to handle the books and I've always been pretty good with numbers. I'm thinking about it. I'm living off my Army retirement right now and some savings I have, but yeah, I'm going to have to figure out something to do at some point—more to keep me busy than for the money. I don't require much to keep me happy, especially living up here."

"You could seriously make those toy blocks into a business—"

"Naw, I do that for fun and to work with Sam. I think sometimes when you turn a hobby into a business, it loses its fun, you know? I guess I sound a little unambitious to a woman who's about to start law school."

"Not at all. I'm happiest when I'm doing yoga. If I could make real money teaching yoga, I would rethink law school."

"So why do you want to go to law school then?" I've been wondering that since I met her. She doesn't seem like that would be something she would enjoy.

"Uhh, because I want to practice law." She shrugs and laughs.

"Try again."

"What? You don't think I can be a lawyer?" she says, folding her arms over her chest.

"That's not what I said—at all. You can be anything you want to be. I just want to know why you're interested in law."

"Oh." She relaxes a little bit and puts her head back on my shoulder. "Everyone except Kit has discouraged me from going. I'm just sensitive about it, I guess."

"I'm not discouraging it. Do you really want to go though? It seems like every time you talk about it, you get kind of edgy." I laugh and kiss the top of her head. "Maybe you should drop out and move up here."

"What?" She leans back defensively.

"Whoa, whoa, Elle," I say, holding my hands up. "I was kidding. Just a stupid joke."

"I just told you that everyone's been trying to discourage me. Why would you say that? And I'm not edgy." She's definitely edgy. "Being a lawyer pays well. And it's steady work if you're good at it."

"Elle, take a breath."

"Stop telling me what to do." She stands up and looks around like someone's chasing her. "Why does everyone want me to move out of L.A.?"

"I'm not telling you what to do." I reach out and take her hand. "I made a stupid joke. That's it. Seriously, I have your back no matter what. And I think we both know if I was telling you what to do, you'd do the exact opposite anyway."

She laughs a little bit and lets me pull her back down to the couch.

"Let me ask it another way," I say, taking a deep breath. "If you had all the money in the world, what would you do?"

"I would give you all of it to stop asking me questions." She smiles, but I can tell she's done with this conversation.

"I will do that for free." I pull her into a hug. "You'll be a great lawyer. And since I made you mad, you get to ask me another question."

She surrenders into the hug. "Same one, if you had all the money in the world, what would you do?"

"Exactly what I'm doing now—talking to you."

Chapter Thirty-Two

NOELLE

December 25
Blitzen Bay, California

"Well, you're an early riser this morning—first one through the door. Merry Christmas, Noelle!"

Gabi's standing behind the bar—drinking a cup of coffee while she reloads napkin dispensers.

"Merry Christmas, Gabi. I've been up pretty much all night. I thought I'd just start the day."

She pours me a cup of coffee as I sit at the bar. "Your fiancé came in here last night looking for you."

"He found me," I say, sighing. "And he's my ex-fiancé now."

Izzy comes through the kitchen door. She looks as tired as I feel.

"Did I hear 'ex-fiancé'?" I swear her hearing's as good as my mom's.

"Yeah, I broke it off for good last night. We're done."

Izzy comes around the bar and hugs me. "I'm sorry, Noelle, but it seems like that was the right decision."

She pushes me back from the hug and covers her face with her hands.

"Are you okay?" I say. "You don't look so good."

She starts massaging her temples. "I have a migraine. I haven't had one in so long. They usually signal something bad is coming. And it's a monster-sized one today. It's giving me anxiety."

"Hmm. Maybe you should go back to bed."

"I would love to, but we give our entire staff Christmas off since we're just open for breakfast. Gabi can't do it alone."

"I'll take your shift. I waitress at a sports bar in L.A. This will be easy."

Gabi walks over and puts her arm around Izzy. "Babe, I think that's a good idea. We're never that busy on Christmas—just the regulars. Go back to bed. Noelle and I can handle it."

Izzy looks unconvinced.

"I'll make you a deal," I say, pushing her gently toward their apartment door. "If you go back to bed, as your Christmas present, you can ask me any question you want and I will answer it completely. You can delve down deep into my soul."

Gabi laughs. "Iz, that's like a pot of gold for you. There's no way you can turn it down."

Izzy has her hands over her face again, trying to block the ray of light flooding through the window. She peeks through her fingers. "Any question? Nothing off the table?"

"Nothing off the table."

She takes off her apron and hands it to me. "My headache feels better already."

Gabi shakes her head as Izzy disappears through the door. "You've done it now. No telling what she's going to come up with—"

"It's all good. I don't mind."

Gabi hands me an order pad. "Head's up, newbie. Your first customer just came in."

I turn around to see Sam smiling at me.

"Merry Christmas, Sam!" I bound across the room and hug him.

"Merry Christmas, Noelle." He takes off his coat to reveal a bright green sweater accented by the collar of a red plaid shirt.

"You look positively festive!" I say as he slides into his normal booth.

"I try to wear all of my red and green clothes at least once in December." He points at the apron as I wrap it around my waist. "Please tell me your new job indicates that you're staying with us in Blitzen Bay."

"Izzy's not feeling well today, so I'm just helping out. What can I get you this morning?"

"Gabi always has my breakfast prepared almost before I sit down," he says, grinning again, "but you can get me a cup of coffee—the first one with caffeine and then the rest unleaded, please."

Gabi's putting a bowl of oatmeal in front of him when I make it back with the coffee.

She looks at me. "What do you want for breakfast? You might as well grab something while it's only Sam here."

"Just a bowl of fruit would be great." I slide in across from Sam and pour myself a cup of coffee. "Do you mind if I eat with you?"

He pushes his newspaper to the wall. "It would be my pleasure. That will make two meals I get to share with you today if you're still coming to my dinner tonight?"

"I wouldn't miss it for the world."

"I hope you like paella. That's what Holly and I always made on Christmas." His eyes dim for a second as he says her name.

I reach over and take his hand. "How long were you and Holly married?"

"A little more than forty years." He's smiling again. "You know we got married three months after we met."

"What? That's amazing," I say as Gabi puts my breakfast down on the table. "Gabi, did you know that?"

"Yeah, it was love at first sight, but who wouldn't fall in love with Sam the minute they saw him." She leans over and kisses him on the head before walking back to the kitchen.

He laughs and then whispers, "Noelle, may I tell you a secret?"

"I love secrets so much," I say, leaning forward.

"Holly's parents didn't like me at all when they met me."

"What?" I fling myself back against the bench. "How's that possible? You're perfect."

"Well, in their defense, I was kind of a mess when we started dating. I had just gotten back from Vietnam and—well, I was a lot to handle. I was mad and grumpy and generally not a lot of fun to be around."

"I can't believe that's true. You said Holly fell in love with you the second she saw you."

"No, I said I fell in love with her at first sight. And really, it wasn't even at first sight. I heard her laugh before I saw her. I was sitting at a bar in San Diego, trying to lose myself in a beer, like I had every night since I got back from 'Nam. All of a sudden I heard this laugh. It went on forever, but in a nice lilting way. It sounded like a song. It was such an interesting sound. I knew I had to find the person responsible. I looked all around the bar and saw her staring at me. When I looked back, she started laughing again. I grinned from ear-to-ear. So much for being subtle, huh?"

"But she was staring at you! Maybe it was love at first sight for her, too."

"No, for her it was intrigue-at-first-sight. She led a pretty sheltered life up to that point—growing up in little Blitzen Bay with very conservative parents. I wasn't like anything she'd ever seen, especially fresh back from the war. I was pretty chaotic—physically and mentally."

"So how long did it take her to fall in love with you? It must have been pretty quick."

"About a month," he says, laughing. "I was a project. She liked projects. That's how it started, but within a month, she saw right through my hard shell to who I truly was. She started pulling that part of me back out gradually. And the rest, as they say, is history."

I sigh. "That's just lovely. Maybe I'll find that one day."

"Maybe you already have—"

"No, I broke it off with my fiancé last night. We're done for good."

He lays his hand on top of mine. "I'm very sorry to hear that, Noelle, but if he wasn't the person for you, I'm also relieved that you didn't marry him. You're a bright light—an absolute ray of sunshine. You deserve someone who not only encourages you to shine but also loves basking in your glow."

"I hope I find him someday."

Sam smiles and nods toward the door. "I think you have a new customer."

I turn around to see Nash standing at the door.

Chapter Thirty-Three

NASH

December 25
Blitzen Bay, California

"So what, you work here now?"

When Elle stands up, I see she's wearing a waitress's apron. She grabs an order pad off Sam's table.

"Izzy had a headache. I told her to go lie down and I'd take her shift." She smiles at me as she makes her way over to my table with a pot of coffee. "And Merry Christmas, by the way."

She has on black leggings tucked into her fur-lined boots. The sleeves on her white T-shirt are pushed up to her elbows. Her hair's back in a messy ponytail with strands falling around her glowing face. She looks like she belongs here.

"Merry Christmas, Elle," I say, smiling as she pours my coffee. "And what do you know about waitressing?"

"I know enough to get the coffee into the cups of people I

like and into the laps of people I don't like. Which do you want to be?" She raises her eyebrows and does that little head tilt that makes me crazy.

"I'd like to stay on your good side, ma'am. Thank you."

"Good choice. Would you like your regular? B&G, scrambled, and coffee, right?"

She writes it down on her pad and walks away without waiting for my reply. I can't help but notice how cute her butt looks in those pants. I watch her for a few minutes as she walks around the bar—serving coffee to a group that walked in behind me. Every person she approaches lights up when she's talking to them. It's like she's the sun spreading her glow from east to west and then back again.

"You're kind of late today," she says, putting my plate in front of me and refilling my coffee. "It's past seven. Did you sleep in?"

"I'm up at five every morning. I'm late because I was looking for you. I stopped by the inn first. I thought maybe you'd left."

"I told you I wasn't leaving the North Pole before Christmas."

"Happy to hear it," I say, looking down at my plate. There's a bowl of blueberries in the middle of my usual breakfast. "Elle, why are there blueberries on my plate?"

"Because they're delicious and they're good for you. You're almost thirty. You need to start eating healthier."

"I'm not almost thirty. I'm almost twenty-seven and I told you I don't like fruit."

"You're in your late twenties. It's a downward slide from here. Oops, hold up. New customer." She pops out of the booth and looks back at me over her shoulder. "Eat your blueberries, grandpa."

She bounces across the floor—her ponytail swinging back and forth. She pours a cup of coffee for Darrel who owns the hardware store down the block. He smiles broadly as he watches her walk away. She puts his order in and makes her way back over to me.

"So, I've never known Izzy to take as much as an hour off. How'd you get her to sit out the entire morning?"

She slides back into the booth. "I promised her she could ask me any question and I would answer it fully and honestly."

"No, Elle," I say, jerking backward like someone just slapped me. "Rookie mistake. You can't give Izzy that kind of power. She already knows way too much about everyone."

She shrugs. "I told you, I'm an open book."

"Oh right. We'll see. I still have a lot more questions I want to ask you."

The "order-up" bell rings from the kitchen. She jumps up again.

"I'll answer anything, but you have to answer more for me." She spins around and smiles at me and turns back around to the kitchen in one fluid motion. "Please have your blueberries eaten by the time I get back."

"So, is our relationship just going to be you bossing me around?" I call after her.

"I mean if that's how you want it to work, I'm totally comfortable with it."

"That's not what I said," I say, smiling at her retreating back.

"That's what I heard!"

I watch her as she grabs Darrel's plate, delivers it to his table, and walks back over to me. She looks down at my plate and sees the untouched blueberries. I shake my head and put a big spoonful into my mouth. They're not too bad.

"Very nice." She sits down again. "So what questions? Ask away—"

"How long were you and Steve together?"

"Two years. We started dating right before my junior year," she says without a hint of sadness in her voice.

"Did you date someone before him?" I eat another helping of the blueberries. She smiles.

"No one serious in college before him, but I had a serious high school boyfriend."

"So you're like a serial monogamist."

She shrugs. "Yeah, I guess. I've never been very good at juggling things. How about you?"

"How about me, what?"

"More monogamist or play the field? Did you have a girlfriend in high school?"

I stroke my beard. "Several."

She rolls her eyes. "Yeah, I kind of had you pictured as a player."

"I'm not a player." I shake my head. "It's just, you know, finding women has never been a problem. Finding the right woman on the other hand . . ."

"Hmm," she says, squinting her eyes. "Who do I think would be the right woman for Nash Young?"

I smile as I finish up the blueberries. "You know my mom told me the other day that I'm a caretaker, so I need someone to take care of, but I told her women don't need me or any guy to take care of them."

"It's the difference between need and want," she says. "We don't need it, but want it? I guess it depends on the woman."

"Okay," I say slowly. "How about you? Is that something you want?"

"The other night before Dad left, he told me to find a man who would always have my back. That kind of care—yeah, I want that a lot. I don't need someone to take care of me financially or even physically, you know? But someone to back me up, to be there for me emotionally, I want that. It's not easy to find a guy who understands the difference."

"You're not looking in the right place—"

"Really?" She locks her eyes with mine and smiles. "Am I looking in the right place now?"

I smile and nod slowly. "Well, I guess that's up to you, but I definitely have your back and you already know my chest is made for hugging, so . . ."

"I have a feeling you'd have a problem with me taking care of myself financially and physically."

"Not at all. In fact, if you want to keep me as your trophy boyfriend, I would be very okay with that. And I've already started getting you ready to kick people's butts, so go crazy."

"Yet every time anyone tries to confront me, you throw me behind you and when I try to pay for something, you steal my credit card. I think you need to take care of people that way."

"Need and want," I say, laughing. "Do I want to take care of you in every way possible? Yes. So much. But I don't need to. I'm okay with boundaries."

She shakes her head and laughs. "See, those blueberries

have already helped your brain function. You're thinking very quickly on your feet."

"Thank God I have you to look after me." I drain the last of my coffee. "What time does your shift end? Do you want to hang out after?"

"You know, I really need to chill today, but I still want to go to Sam's tonight. Are you going to pick me up?"

I try not to show my disappointment. I'm getting used to being around her all day. "Yeah, of course. Around five-thirty?"

"Perfect." She stands up and points at my empty bowl. "Good work with the blueberries. You feel younger, don't you?"

"At least ten years," I say, laughing as I watch her walk away.

For the first time since she got here, I realize that this is temporary. She's leaving tomorrow. A wave of desperation runs through my body.

Chapter Thirty-Four

NOELLE

December 25
Blitzen Bay, California

"Wow," Nash says as I walk down the stairs. "You look gorgeous."

Kit brought some clothes from my apartment including a deep red, knit wrap dress with a plunging neckline. She always seems to know what I need. I thought it might be a little too much for tonight, but from the look on Nash's face, I think I nailed it.

"Thanks." I stop on the last step and smile at him as he walks over to me. "You look gorgeous, too."

He's wearing jeans with a slightly fitted, gray pullover. The sweater outlines his chest muscles perfectly. I'm trying very unsuccessfully to stop staring at them.

He smiles. "I look gorgeous, huh? I think that's the first time anyone has ever told me that."

"Well, they obviously weren't looking at you clearly."

He offers me his hand as I walk down the last step.

"I'm not nearly as festive as you," he says, looking down at my dress. "I don't have any red in my wardrobe."

"Well, it's a good thing I'm your date then," I say, pulling a Santa hat out of my bag. "I bought it at the store yesterday."

"Really?" He raises his eyebrows. "And how did you buy anything when I still have your credit card?"

"Someone better keep an eye on his wallet." I tilt my head and smile.

"Very sneaky," he says. He looks down at the Santa hat. "You know, my first instinct is to say no, but I think I might look good in that."

He takes the hat and adjusts it on his head—flipping the pom-pom to the back. "What do you think?"

"It's perfect. You'll be the most festive person there."

"Hmm," he says, shaking his head. The pom-pom slaps him in the face. "Let's go before I change my mind."

I sit down on the bench at the front door and grab my snow boots.

"I'm not sure these boots vibe with the dress."

He kneels and takes them from me. "I think they look perfect. Here, I'll tie them for you."

"If you keep doing this, I'm going to forget how to put on my shoes. You're spoiling me."

"That's the idea." He looks up for a second and smiles at me.

I lean back on the wall and look at him—down on his knees in front of me. It almost looks like he's proposing. A tingling sensation shoots through my body. I take a deep breath.

"You okay?" he says as he finishes tying the laces.

"Yeah, not sure where I went there," I say as he grabs my coat off the rack. When he gets it on me, he reaches under my hair and pulls it out of the coat. It makes me tingle again. I turn around quickly and try to zip my coat up. My hands aren't working.

"I'll get it." He zips it up to my chin and lets his hands linger on my shoulders for a second. "What's wrong?"

I look up at him. "I'm trying to envision Steve doing this."

He takes a quick step closer to me, so our bodies are just touching.

"I'm not Steve," he says, his voice deep and husky. "And I can prove that to you in a hundred different ways. You just let me know when you want me to start."

He guides my hands up and rests them on his chest. He's looking down at me—his eyes are gentle, but his body is hungry. I know he can feel me starting to tremble. We stand there, looking into each other's eyes, for what seems like an eternity. I don't think I'm breathing.

"C'mon," he says softly. "We're already late."

He moves away from me but keeps hold of one of my hands. He pulls me toward the door. I feel like my mind has temporarily quit working. I can't think of anything to say.

He opens the truck door for me and gives me his hand to help me in. I can't stop staring at him. He smiles at me as he closes my door. When he gets in, I still haven't fastened my seatbelt. He reaches over me, grabs it, and clicks it into place.

As he's scooting over to his side, he pauses and places a soft kiss on my lips. I take a shaky breath as he pulls back.

"That's just a deposit," he says, looking at me. "Let me know when you're ready for more."

I nod and look down. He smiles and starts talking about something. I have no idea what he's saying. I'm not replying. I'm struggling to form a word in my mouth. When we arrive, he opens my door and stops me before I get out of the truck. He pulls me into a hug.

"Breathe. It can be something or nothing," he whispers into my ear. "You know where I stand, but I'm in no hurry. I'll wait forever if I have to, okay?"

I nod against his chest. When he tries to back up, I won't let him go. My arms are still around his neck. His face is inches from mine.

"I think I want it to be something—"

Before I even get the words out, his mouth is on mine. His arms circle back around me and pull me tightly into him. I'm still sitting in the truck. He's moved his body so it's pressed between my legs. My fingers weave through his hair as he pushes against me—kissing me hungrily.

The feeling of his body pressed against me makes me moan. He moves his head back an inch—pulling gently on my bottom lip. We're both panting like we've just sprinted a mile.

"My house is right there," he growls, nodding his head backward. "Maybe we should go there first."

He kisses me again. He's holding me so tightly that I'm starting to feel a little faint.

"You might have to help me over there," I say as I nibble on his ear. "I'm not sure I can walk right now."

"I'll carry you if you need me to—"

"Hey! Are you guys coming in, or are you waiting for an invitation?"

We both jump back a little when we hear Gabi's voice coming from Sam's house. She must see the back of the truck. There's no way she can see us.

Nash takes a deep breath. "To be continued?"

I nod and smile as he kisses me gently one more time and then takes my hand to help me down.

"We're coming!" Nash yells. "Elle's finishing up a phone call."

As we walk around the retaining wall, Gabi, Izzy, and Sam smile at us from the front door.

"Come in! Come in!" Sam says, motioning us forward. "Izzy and Gabi just got here."

Nash takes my hand and guides me up the sidewalk. Just the feeling of his hand against mine makes my head start spinning again. He looks back at me and smiles as he laces his fingers into mine.

The warmth of Sam's house snaps me back into focus. Everywhere I look, there are pictures of his kids, grandkids, and a beautiful woman who must be Holly.

"I love your house, Sam," I say, hugging him. "It's as warm and lovely as you are."

"It looks much better with you in it," he says, smiling. "I'm so glad I get to spend my Christmas with you."

Nash leads me into the kitchen. Gabi and Izzy look down at our firmly joined hands. Their expressions make me a little self-conscious. I try to pull my hand away, but Nash holds it tighter.

"Nash," Gabi says, pointing at his head, "I can't imagine you own a Santa hat. Was that a gift?"

"Yeah, Elle gave it to me," he says, pulling me in front of him as he leans back on the counter. "Looks good, right?"

"With Noelle's dress, you look very couple-y." Izzy does a quick scan of us.

Nash shakes his head. "Iz, quit trying to dig."

"I'm just saying." Izzy looks at Sam. "Sammy, can I play in Holly's jewelry a little before dinner?"

"Of course, dear." Sam smiles at her. "You know where it is."

Izzy grabs my hand. "Noelle, come with me. I want to show it to you."

Nash puts his arms around my waist and pulls back on me. "She's not going anywhere with you, nosy."

Izzy holds my hand firmly. "I believe Miss Noelle owes me something and it's time to collect."

"I know about your little deal with her," Nash says, "and she doesn't have to answer any questions for you."

"Nash, it's fine," I say, moving his arms from around me. I smile back at him as I let Izzy pull me away.

"Five minutes and then I'm coming to rescue you. What do you want to drink?"

"Red wine, please," I say as we disappear around the corner.

Izzy pulls me into a woman's dressing room. It looks like Sam hasn't touched it since Holly died. There's still a table filled with perfumes and lotions. Izzy takes a jewelry box out of the closet and sits down on the bright pink tufted couch.

"Noelle, come and sit next to me," she says, patting the couch cushion. "I think you owe me something."

I laugh as I sit down next to her. "I do. Ask away, girl. Any question is fine."

"What are your intentions for Nash?"

Her unyielding tone makes me jump a little bit.

"My intentions?" I'm trying to stall because I know I don't have an answer.

"Yes, Noelle, your intentions. I would have to be blind not to pick up on the chemistry between you two, but as much as I like you, I love him and I don't want him to get hurt. He's obviously crazy about you, but I'm guessing you're not in a place to return that right now."

"Uh," I say, hesitating. "I told you I would be honest, so my answer is that I don't know. I'm sorry I can't give you more but that's the truth. I really don't know."

She pats my hand. "I know you're being honest and I appreciate that, but your answer makes me worry about him even more. I don't want him to get hurt. I don't want either of you to get hurt. Maybe just cool it since you're leaving tomorrow."

I take a deep breath as Nash walks into the room.

Chapter Thirty-Five

NASH

December 25
Blitzen Bay, California

"She's something else, huh?"

Gabi hands me two wine glasses as I reach for the open bottle of red.

"Who? Elle?" I say, looking away from her as I pour.

"You know who I'm talking about, Nash," Gabi says impatiently. "You haven't taken your eyes off her all week. Or your hands."

On the way to pick up Elle tonight, I promised myself I would back off. I'm sensing that she's not ready. But that promise blew up the minute she walked down the staircase at the Holly House. She's wearing a clingy, low-cut red dress that accentuates every inch of her ample curves perfectly. It was everything I could do not to carry her right back up the stairs into her bed.

I keep my eyes fixed on the wine glasses. My face starts to get hot. "Yeah, she seems great."

"Really? 'She seems great.' That's all you've got?" Gabi leans against the island and crosses her arms as she stares at me.

I look up at her. "I mean, what else do you want me to say? She's not even twenty-four hours out of an engagement. She's not exactly available."

"I was wondering if you realized that. Seems like you're getting in a little deep—"

"I'm not. I'm fine. We're just friends. I'm taking her back to L.A. tomorrow. We might never see each other again."

That thought's been running through my mind all afternoon, but saying it out loud makes me start to panic a little bit.

Gabi pats my back. "As long as you realize that. I don't want you to get hurt."

"Quit worrying about me. I'm fine," I say, picking up the glasses as I head back to find Elle.

"You're my family," Gabi says as I walk away. "I'm never going to quit worrying about you."

I walk down the hall until I hear voices coming out of a room in the back. When I walk in, Izzy's looking at Elle like a prosecutor trying to get an answer out of a witness.

"What? What's going on?" I look quickly from Izzy to Elle.

"Nothing's going on, Nash," Izzy says. "Just girl talk."

"Hmm." I hand Elle the wine and put my hand on her shoulder. "I don't think I like that."

Elle pats my hand. "It's all good. Izzy, I heard what you said. Thank you for saying it."

"What'd she say?" I look at Izzy sternly.

Elle takes my hand and starts leading me out of the room. I don't budge.

"Izzy? What'd you say?" I repeat.

"Now who's being nosy," Elle says, pulling on my hand harder. "C'mon, let's see if Sam needs help with dinner."

When we get in the hall, I pull back on her hand and stop her. "Tell me what she said."

"It's not a big deal. She doesn't want you to get hurt. It's sweet—the equivalent of what Kit said to you about me. We're lucky we have people who care about us so much."

"I'm a grown man, Elle." I put my hands on her shoulders and look directly into her eyes. "Izzy did not need to say that. I'm not going to get hurt and I'm definitely not going to hurt you. That should be the furthest thing from your mind. Okay?"

She smiles and nods as I lean down and kiss her. She doesn't kiss me back.

"This is about me and you," I say, pulling her into a hug. "Not Izzy, not Kit, not Steve. Just me and you."

"Okay," she whispers.

I put my arm around her protectively as we walk into the kitchen. Sam and Gabi have started putting food on the table.

"Hey, will you help Sam finish with the table?" Gabi says, smiling at us. "I'll go tear my wife away from Holly's jewelry."

By the time they get back, Sam, Elle, and I are seated at the table with plates of food steaming all around us. Elle's sitting between Sam and me. I have my hand resting on her leg under the table.

"Do you mind if I say grace?" Sam smiles at us as he

continues, "Thank you, God, for bringing this family together tonight. We thank you for old friends and praise you for bringing new friends into the fold. May our loved ones who are no longer with us bless this gathering with peace and fill it with their love and compassion. Amen."

When I look up, Elle's holding Sam's hand.

"Peace and compassion," she says, smiling at him. "That's the perfect combination at Christmas."

"'Glory to God in the highest, and on earth peace, good will toward men,'" Sam says, smiling back at her.

"Right! That's from Charlie Brown's Christmas," Elle exclaims.

Sam's eyes light up. "Well, I think it was in the Bible first, but yes, Linus did an excellent job of reciting it. That was my kid's favorite Christmas show—mine, too."

"That's the one we watched first every year at my grandma's house. It's my favorite memory of Christmas."

"Is your grandma still with us?" Sam says as he starts dishing out paella onto the waiting plates.

"No, she died four years ago." She pauses. I squeeze her leg gently. "All of my grandparents are gone."

"Not all of them," Sam says as he puts her plate in front of her. "I've been looking for another granddaughter if you'll let me adopt you."

She beams at him. "It would be my honor."

I put my arm around her and squeeze her shoulder as I start digging into my meal.

"So Elle, you're leaving tomorrow, right?" Gabi says, looking directly at me.

"Uh, yeah," Elle says, jumping a little bit at the harsh tone in Gabi's voice. "I need to get back to L.A. I start law school in a few weeks."

"Oh no," Sam says. "That makes me so sad. I'm not sure why I thought we got to keep you in Blitzen Bay. Will you promise to visit us? I don't get down to L.A. anymore."

Elle smiles and pats his hand. "Of course, I will visit you, but when I graduate, I want you to come to L.A. for my ceremony. I want all my favorite people there."

"I wouldn't miss it, Noelle. What kind of law will you be studying?"

"I'm starting with international law. My undergrad degree is in international studies. I guess I'll see where that takes me."

"Pepperdine, right?" Gabi looks at Elle this time. "Do you live close to campus?"

Elle takes a deep breath. "Uh, as of last week, I lived with Steve in an apartment near UCLA. I'm not sure where I'm going to live now."

"Is he still living there?" Izzy looks at me.

"Could we maybe stop grilling her?" I say as I feel Elle's leg tense up under my hand. Although, I'd like to know the answer to that last question, too.

"It's fine," Elle says, smiling at me. "I don't know if he's still living there. I guess I'll find out tomorrow."

"We'll find out," I say under my breath.

Elle looks up at me.

I continue quietly. "When I take you back there tomorrow. We'll find out. If you need to move into a hotel or something temporarily, we can work it out."

She smiles and nods, but her eyes are wide and hesitant. A

wave of panic starts rising in my body again. For the rest of the meal, everyone's telling stories about their Christmas traditions growing up. I force myself to tell the story about my family trips to a Christmas tree farm, but I've stopped paying attention to the conversation. The reality of Elle leaving tomorrow is hitting home and it's hitting home hard.

Chapter Thirty-Six
NOELLE

December 25
Blitzen Bay, California

"Sam, will you show me pictures of Holly and your kids after we finish cleaning up?"

I'm desperate to get my mind on anything else but the way Nash's hand felt on my thigh all through dinner. It was distracting enough when his hand was resting near my knee, but as the wine kept flowing, his hand got more active. While we were eating dessert, he started rubbing his hand gently up and down my leg until he finally let it rest in the fold between my thigh and stomach. I genuinely thought I was going to pass out.

"We'll do the dishes," Izzy says, pointing at Gabi and Nash. "You two look at pictures."

Sam takes my hand and leads me to the couch where he grabs a well-worn photo album from under the table. He spends the next twenty minutes leafing through the pages—pointing out every member of his lovely family.

Nash makes it over to us after the dishes are done and sits on the other side of me—his hand going back on my leg. We're just getting to a section that looks like Sam's days in the military.

"Who's that?" I point to a picture of a very young Sam with his arm around another soldier. They both have rifles slung over their shoulders and big, cheesy grins on their faces.

"That was my best friend," Sam says, smiling as he touches the picture gently.

"He's gone now?" I reach out and hold Sam's hand.

"He's been gone for a long time. He died in the war."

Nash's leg tenses against mine. I put my hand on top of his. It's shaking. I squeeze it as I hear him take a long, labored breath. I keep my eyes on Sam.

"I'm sorry, Sam. What was his name?"

"Jack."

"He was very handsome," I say, looking back down at the picture.

Nash squeezes my leg hard—too hard. I pat his hand a few times without looking at him. He releases my leg and pulls his hand away.

"Yeah, he was," Sam laughs. "The ladies flocked around him. And he was so funny—always had some ridiculous story to tell. I was his best audience. I couldn't quit laughing when we were together."

Nash stands up suddenly. "I need to get some fresh air."

I look up at him. His face is pale. His eyes are shifting around the room.

"Are you okay?" I say, reaching for his hand, but he takes a step back.

He looks away quickly. "Yeah, yeah, I'm good. I'll be right back."

I start to follow him, but Sam takes my arm.

"Give him a second," he says, smiling at me.

Gabi and Izzy come into the room. Their eyes follow Nash outside. They exchange concerned looks.

"Sam, we need to head out," Izzy says. "We've got some stuff to do to get the bar ready for breakfast in the morning. Thank you so much for dinner. The paella was amazing. We're going to have to hire you as a cook in the bar."

"Any time. I loved spending my Christmas with you."

Gabi puts her hand on Izzy's shoulder. "Sam, I checked her pockets to make sure she didn't steal any of Holly's jewelry."

"I've told you before, you're welcome to any of it, Isabelle." Sam closes the photo album and pushes himself slowly up from the couch. "I think you enjoy it as much as Holly did."

"No, I can't take any of it. Those are good memories of her."

"I'm going to give you something in my will anyway," Sam says, trying to muffle a yawn. "You might as well take it now."

Izzy hugs him again. "Well, since you're never going to die, I'm never going to get it. And I wouldn't have it any other way."

I stand up. "I should go, too. Thank you so much for a wonderful Christmas."

Sam hugs me. "Do you promise to come and see me?"

"I promise," I say, kissing his cheek. "And I want to see more of these pictures the next time."

I grab Nash's coat as we walk out. He's standing on the porch, staring out toward the lake. He looks over at us.

"Is the party breaking up?" He looks right at me.

"Yeah," Izzy says. "We'll take Noelle back to the inn."

He walks over and takes my hand. "No, it's good. I can take her back."

"That doesn't make any sense." Izzy grabs my arm.

I pull it away. "You know, it's such a nice night. I think I'll walk. I need to work off those Christmas cookies anyway."

Izzy stares back and forth from Nash to me a few times before Gabi grabs her. "Okay, we're going home. Merry Christmas to both of you. Noelle, make sure you say goodbye before you head back to L.A."

"I will." I hug both of them. "Merry Christmas."

"I'm going to tell Sam goodbye," Nash says as we watch them get in their car. "Wait here for me."

When he comes back out, he takes my hand and leads me down the sidewalk toward his house. I pull back on him as we reach the driveway.

"What's wrong?" He turns around. I'm standing a few steps higher than him, so we're face-to-face.

"Nash—"

"Elle, it's fine," he says, putting his arms around my waist. "If the moment's passed, it's passed. I told you I'm not in a hurry. If you're not ready, it's fine."

"My body's ready—like really ready," I say as he pulls me closer to him, "but my mind isn't there yet. It's just—"

"You don't have to explain," he whispers as he pulls me into a hug. "You never have to explain what you're feeling. If you're feeling it, it's the right thing."

"The right thing for who?"

He pulls his head back and looks right into my eyes. "For you. It's the right thing for you and that's all that should matter to you. Everyone else can take care of themselves, including me."

I take a deep breath and nod. He helps me down the final few steps to the driveway.

"Do you want to go back to the inn?" he asks, putting his arm around me.

"I think I should go back." My words sound as sad as I feel, but my gut's screaming at me that it's the right thing. It hasn't failed me yet. I guess I need to keep listening to it.

"Okay, I'll take you back." He kisses the top of my head as he starts guiding me toward his truck.

"Do you mind if we walk back? It's so pretty out tonight."

"Not at all," he says, smiling as he takes my hand. "I get to spend more time with you that way."

Chapter Thirty-Seven

NASH

December 25
Blitzen Bay, California

"What time do you want me to take you back tomorrow?"

My tone's unintentionally harsh. I'm distracted. My body's settled down, but my mind's still on Mikey. Hearing Sam talk about his buddy who died in Vietnam brought it all back up for me with a ferocity that I haven't felt for a while.

Elle's head snaps up to look at me.

"Uh, maybe you shouldn't take me back," she says slowly. "I can call a car service or something."

"No, Elle. I'm sorry. My mind's on something else. That came out wrong."

She puts her hand on my arm. "I know. It's fine, but really, maybe it's not a good idea."

"What?" I stop walking. "No, I'm taking you back."

"It's just—you know—if Steve's still in the apartment, it's going to be weird—"

"He'll get over it." I put my hands on her shoulders and pull her closer. "I don't want you alone with him after what I witnessed last night."

She looks down. "He won't hurt me—not physically. I mean, he might yell at me a little bit more, but I can handle that."

"Elle, please just let me protect you from that." My voice sounds tense. I try to even it out. "You shouldn't have to deal with it alone."

"Okay." She smiles and nods, but she still doesn't look convinced.

I take her hand and start walking again. We walk for a few more minutes in silence.

"What was his name?" She's looking up at me—her eyes wide and glassy.

"Whose name?"

"The friend you lost in the Army," she whispers.

My body freezes. "Did Sam tell you that?"

"No. I could just tell. When he started talking about his friend who died, your whole body tensed up."

I nod but don't say anything. I take her hand and start walking. I'm waiting for my body to start panicking again. Nothing happens.

"Mikey," I say, finally. "Mike Anders."

"I'm sorry, Nash." She squeezes my hand.

"So am I. He was a good guy." I motion to a bench in front of the hardware store. "Do you mind if we sit for a second?"

She sits next to me and lays her head on my shoulder.

"What was he like?"

My body still feels calm. "Uh, he was quiet. You know, one of those guys who doesn't have much to say, but when he says something, you know you better listen because it's important."

Amazingly, my mind feels calm, too. It hasn't felt this way once when I've thought about him. I feel a sudden urge to talk about him more.

"And he was hopeful—you know? With what we saw in our jobs, it was easy to get bitter, but he always found the good side. Kind of like you." I add, "The hopeful part, not the quiet part."

She laughs. "Understood."

"I got kind of surly when we were over there too long. Mikey always knew how to cheer me up. And he didn't even do anything, you know? Just having him around put me in a better mood. Again, like you."

She smiles. "He sounds like he was a great guy. I wish I could have known him."

"Yeah, you would have liked him and he would have loved you," I say, laughing. "He was into blondes."

"Is that right?" she says, her eyes lighting up. "And how did he do with the blondes?"

"He did very well. The ladies like the strong, silent type."

"Yes, we do." She nuzzles back into my chest.

"How long has he been gone?"

"Exactly a year on the day of your wedding."

She sits up quickly and looks at me with her mouth gaping open.

"Oh my God, Nash. That day had to be so hard for you

already and then I pulled you into my nonsense. I feel awful. I'm so sorry."

"Don't be sorry. You saved me. I wasn't sure I was going to make it through that day and then when you crawled into my truck. I forgot about him entirely."

"And that's a good thing?"

"Yeah, the last thing he would want is for me to be miserable," I take her hands, "especially with a good-looking blonde around."

She laughs again. "Somehow, I don't think he would have approved of the blonde being the bride at the wedding."

"Ah, Mikey didn't care much about rules. Not only would he have approved of me going after you, he would have run interference so I could have a clearer path."

"He sounds like Kit. She's always been my enabler."

"You know, on the surface, they have nothing in common, but Mikey always had my back just like Kit has yours."

"I want to see a picture of him if you have one."

I take a quick breath. I haven't been able to even look at a picture of him since he died. I slowly pull out my phone.

"Let me see if I can find one," I say as I start flipping through my Army pictures.

I find one of him smiling like an idiot with his arm around a llama. I remember taking that picture like it was yesterday. I hand the phone to Elle.

She smiles. "He was so cute. And his blonde friend, too."

"Believe me, that was not the kind of blonde he liked. I think that llama spit at him after I took the picture."

"Where was this?" She zooms in on the picture. I look at his face clearly for the first time in over a year.

"Afghanistan, probably about a year before he was killed." My voice shakes a little bit.

She hands my phone back and burrows into my chest again. "I'm sorry he's not here anymore."

"So am I." I lay my head on top of hers. "You know, that's the first time I've talked about him to anyone since he died. It felt kind of good."

She opens her arms. "Do you need a hug? My chest isn't as broad or huggable as yours, but it's here if you need it."

"Yep, I do. Come here," I say as I pull her onto my lap, facing me. She straddles my legs and wraps her arms around my neck tightly.

"I will hug you as long as you want," she whispers into my ear.

"Well, in that case, we're pretty much going to be sleeping like this tonight."

We sit on the bench, hugging silently for a few minutes. For some reason, it feels like she's saying goodbye. I push her back a little bit and kiss her. She returns it for a second but then pushes her head away from me.

"Nash—"

I put my hands on her face and try to pull her in for another kiss. She presses her hands lightly against my chest.

"I'm sorry," she says, not meeting my gaze.

I lay my forehead against hers. "I told you not to apologize. You know how I feel about you, but if you don't feel the same way—"

"It's not that," she says, climbing off me. She stands up and looks toward the inn. "It's just . . . I'm not ready. I thought I was, but I'm not. It's not fair to you."

"Don't worry about me." I take her hand and start leading her across the street to the inn. "I'm fine. You can have all the time you need. I told you I don't want to be your rebound. If you're not ready to try this, then we wait."

She climbs up on the first step going to the inn and turns around to face me. "Nash, thank you so much for everything you've done for me this week."

"You can thank me tomorrow when I drop you off in L.A."

She nods again but looks down. I tilt her chin up and give her one more gentle kiss.

"Merry Christmas, Elle. I'll see you tomorrow, okay?"

She wraps her arms around me. When she starts to pull back, it takes every bit of strength I have to let her go. She smiles up at me—her eyes full of tears.

"Merry Christmas, Nash."

Chapter Thirty-Eight

NOELLE

December 26
Los Angeles, California

"Are you going to say anything?"

Lola picked me up at the inn about thirty minutes ago. We're at least halfway back to my apartment. I haven't said anything the entire trip.

"What?" I say, looking over at her for the first time. I've been staring down at my lap.

"You told me when you texted last night that you weren't upset about breaking up with Steve." She reaches over and takes my hand. "You seem pretty upset."

"Oh," I say, shaking my head. "This isn't about Steve. Uh, I met someone in Blitzen Bay."

"Really? Okay. And this sadness is about him?"

I rub my hand over my face and sigh. "I'm not sure. I'm so confused right now. Can we not talk about it?"

"Yes, for now, but when you're ready, we're going to talk about it, okay?"

I nod and smile at her. "Tell me about Howie's parents' anniversary party."

"Oh, girl," she says, laughing. "It was horrible."

She's laughing and telling me about his relatives. I'm nodding and smiling at the appropriate times, but I'm not hearing a word she's saying. I'm thinking about Nash.

After last night, I tossed and turned all night in bed. I couldn't think straight. I wanted to run to his house and jump into bed with him and never leave. It excited me. It scared me. It made my mind way more muddled.

Despite trying to think of every way to avoid it, I knew I had to leave Blitzen Bay and get back to L.A. Although I don't want to be alone, I know I need some time to myself to get my mind clear again. I should have told Nash I was leaving, but I ran out just like I did with Steve. I've never run out on anything in my entire life and now I've run out on two guys in the past week. At least this time, I left a note.

"Noelle?" Lola's shaking my arm. "Do you want me to come upstairs with you?"

I suddenly realize we're in my apartment parking lot.

"No, no. I'm good." I smile as I pull her in for a hug. "I really appreciate you coming to get me, Lo, especially the day after Christmas. It's just way above and beyond the rules of the friendship code."

She's squinting her eyes as she taps her fingers on her lips. "I don't like this. I've never seen you this out of it. I'm worried about you."

"I'm fine." I try to smile. "It's been a long week. I need to curl up in bed and get some sleep."

"Okay," she says slowly. "I'll leave, but I want your cousin's phone number first. What's her name? Kat?"

"Kit. Why do you want her number?"

"Because she seems to be your biggest support system. I'm going to need to run your recovery plan through her for approval."

"My what?"

She puts her hand on my shoulder. "Sweetie, I know you did the right thing and you know you did the right thing, but it's still a traumatic event and you're going to crash. That's normal. Crash as hard as you need to, but then we're going to need to start putting the pieces back together. I'm here for you. Kit's here. We'll figure it out together, okay?"

I nod. "I'll text you her number. Maybe we can do a group text to talk about how screwed up my life is right now."

"You're going to be fine. Just get some rest to start with—maybe yoga this weekend."

I stand in the parking lot and wave to her as she drives away. I look up at the second-floor balcony that attaches to our apartment. I guess Steve took the patio furniture that used to be there. He bought it, so I guess that's fair. He can have it. I'm glad I bought the bed and the couch because I need about two days straight of just sleep.

When I open the apartment door, all I see is an empty room. I think I have the wrong apartment for a second until I look down and see my yoga mat, rolled up in the basket by the door. That's all that's in the living room—no couch, no rugs, no tables, no pictures. It looks like the Whos' house after the Grinch empties them of everything.

I walk down the hall and peek into our bedroom. It's empty, too, except for a few wires that hang from the wall where the TV used to be. The tears start rolling down my cheeks. I open my closet. It looks untouched. I open Steve's. It's packed from floor-to-ceiling with our wedding gifts.

I reach out and touch one of the boxes—an air fryer. I stare at it for a minute before I sink to the ground. My body starts shaking. The tears start pouring down my face. I crawl back into the living room and unroll my yoga mat. I curl up and cover myself with the coat Nash bought me.

Chapter Thirty-Nine

NASH

December 26
Blitzen Bay, California

"Hey, Claire. Is Elle up yet? I swear she sleeps later than anyone I know."

When I left last night, Elle said she would text me when she woke up. It's almost eleven.

"Hey, Nash," Claire says with none of her usual enthusiasm. "She didn't tell you she was leaving, did she?"

My heart stops beating for a second.

"What? She left? How? She doesn't have a car."

"Some woman picked her up—"

"Blue hair?"

"No, not the woman from the other night. This woman had black hair—all in braids. I think she said her name was Lola or Lana. It was early—before I had my coffee."

My face must reflect the shock that's surging through my

body because Claire walks quickly over to me and throws her arms around me.

"She didn't tell you," she says, her voice shaking. "Oh, Nash."

"Uhh, no, she didn't tell me." I barely manage to get the words out. "It's . . . it's fine."

I push Claire back and try to smile. She walks over to the front desk and grabs an envelope.

"She left this for you, but I really thought you knew she was leaving. You two seemed to be getting so close."

I run my finger across my name on the envelope.

"Thanks, Claire." I force a smile again.

"I'm so mad at her, Nash—"

"No, she didn't do anything wrong. It's my fault. I pushed her too hard." I turn toward the door. "I need to get going."

She grabs my hand. "I insist you join us for dinner later. We have some friends in town. Come over around three for drinks. We're going to eat around five."

I squeeze her hand. "Thank you, but I have plans. I'll see you around."

"Nash—"

She's saying something as I walk out the door, but I don't turn around. I look at the big Christmas tree, shake my head hard, and then get quickly into my truck.

I throw the envelope on my dashboard. It hits something and makes a pinging noise as it slides to the windshield. I lift the envelope and see one of Elle's hairpins. I pick it up and stare at it for a few minutes before I open the envelope.

. . .

Nash,

I'm sorry for leaving without saying goodbye. This isn't a good excuse, but truly, if I looked into your eyes one more time, I don't think I'd ever be able to leave this place—to leave you. And I have to leave. I have to get back to reality.

I need time. I don't know how much. I have to find myself again and I have to do it alone.

Thank you for saving me in every way possible. I won't blame you if you never want to see me again, but you will forever be one of my favorite people on earth.

Love,
Elle

For the first time since I was a kid, I feel my eyes start to water. In the past year, with everything I've gone through with Mikey, I didn't cry once. Now, I can't hold the tears back. I'm trying my hardest to stop them, but they're rolling down my face like a raging river.

I think about calling her, but I know I can't. I've already pushed her too much. I have to give her the time she needs. I read the note again, take a deep breath, and shove it in the glove compartment with all the Kleenex I bought for her.

When I get back home, I sit in my truck, staring at the lake. I don't even know what to do. Without me realizing it, my life's changed completely in the last four days. I went from wanting to be alone to never wanting to be without Elle again. In my hard, skeptical soul, I didn't think it was possible to feel this way about anyone or anything. And I certainly didn't believe in love at first sight. But now I know what I've been trying to avoid thinking about for the last few days is true: I'm in love with her. I'm deeply in love with her.

I'm a man of action. I go after what I want, but in this case, I can't do anything. The ball's firmly in her court. When I finally drag myself out of the truck, I head down the hill. I grab a few logs, put them on the block, and start chopping. It looks like my woodpile is about to get a lot bigger.

Epilogue

NOELLE

January 20
Los Angeles, California

"Hey, you want to be in my study group? You're the hottest girl in the class. If we don't know the answers, maybe you can flirt them out of the professor."

The guy who's been leering at me since I walked into the auditorium has finally gotten up the nerve to say something. He chose the wrong thing. I'm putting my laptop back in my bag as he starts to sit down next to me.

"Don't ever talk to me again," I say, flipping the stadium seat up so he lands awkwardly on it and falls forward—almost going over into the row in front of us.

He stands up as quickly as he can and looks down at me. "That was meant as a compliment."

"And you're still talking to me," I say, dismissing him with my hand. "Walk away."

He shakes his head and whispers 'bitch' under his breath as he walks down the auditorium stairs.

The woman in front of me turns around—her eyebrows raised. "We're in the middle of a law school. To start with, you would think that he could call you a woman, not a girl, and then maybe say 'you're the smartest woman in the room.'"

"I'd settle for him saying nothing at all," I say, laughing as I fling my backpack over my shoulder.

She laughs and nods her head. "I'm guessing he didn't have much of a chance whatever he said."

She's definitely got that right. I've been back from Blitzen Bay for almost a month and Nash is still the only guy on my mind. Frankly, he's the only thing on my mind most days. I haven't talked to him. I doubt he wants much to do with me after I ran out on him. Despite missing him desperately, I'm starting to feel happier again. Today's my first day of law school. It feels like the step I needed to finally turn the page on the wedding.

After I got back from Blitzen Bay, I didn't move off the yoga mat for a full day. Kit got suspicious when I didn't answer her calls. She mobilized Lola to check on me and then they took over. Kit reserved a hotel room for me and ordered room service every day. She made me sit with her on FaceTime to make sure I ate it. Some days, she would stay on the phone with me as I fell asleep.

While she was babysitting me, Lola found a studio apartment near campus. It's the size of a postage stamp, but it's fully furnished and cheap. And it's really cozy—just what I need right now. I finally got enough energy to return all the wedding presents. I even wrote a few thank you/apology notes. I'm still not fully healed, but I'm getting there.

As I walk out of the building, I close my eyes and inhale the smell of the ocean. The sun's shining down and there's just a little breeze. I'm thinking about taking an hour on the beach before I have to start studying tonight.

When I open my eyes, I see Nash sitting on the wall in front of me. He's wearing shorts, flipflops, and a white T-shirt that's showing off those beautiful arms. I think he might be a mirage until he holds up two coffee cups.

"Is that peppermint hot chocolate?" I say, smiling as I walk over to him.

"Latte with four shots," he says as he hands it to me. "I thought you might need something a little stronger for your first day of school."

"Bless you. I need all the coffee." I take a long sip as I lean on the wall next to him. "Wait, how did you know it was my first day?"

"Kit called me. She's worried that you won't make any friends on your first day."

I shake my head and laugh. "She's been worried about that since the day I started kindergarten. She was in first grade at the same school. She walked out of her classroom—without asking the teacher's permission—and came to my room. She insisted that she sit with me for my first day and refused to move."

He laughs. "Yep, that sounds like Kit."

"She's been more of a mom to me than my actual mother has ever been."

He looks right at me. His eyes are the softest I've ever seen them. "Have you talked to your parents?"

"I've talked to Dad a couple of times," I say, trying unsuccessfully to hold his stare. "Mom still doesn't want to talk to me."

"She'll get over it."

"Maybe." I shrug. "I guess that's up to her."

"So did you make any friends today?" He looks down at his feet. "I'm going to have to report back to Kit or she's going to come after me."

"Well, some pervert told me I was the hottest *girl* in the room, but other than that, no. Law students aren't known for befriending each other."

"You want to point out that pervert to me," he says, looking around at the other students scattered in front of the building. "I'd like to have a little word with him."

"I think I got my point across to him."

"Hmm," he says, looking back at me. "So no other friends, huh?"

"Nope."

"Well, then it's a good thing I came down here, so you would have at least one friend."

I take a deep breath. "Is that what we are now? Friends?"

"Is that what you want to be?" He looks up. The softness is gone. His eyes are as intense as his voice.

"I'm sorry I left without telling you. That was immature. It was just a lot, but I don't have a good excuse."

"You don't need one and you don't have to apologize. It was my fault."

"No, it wasn't," I say. "I was giving you all kinds of mixed signals—"

"You didn't do anything wrong, Elle."

"Neither did you."

"I don't know. You made it pretty clear you didn't want to start something and I kept coming after you anyway."

"Nash, c'mon," I say, draining the last of my latte. "You know I wanted you to kiss me. I wanted you to do a lot more than that to me."

"Excuse me?" He laughs as I walk over to the trash can with my cup. "Wait, come back over here. Will you be really specific about the other things you wanted me to do to you? Just in case I ever get a chance. I want to make sure I'm getting them right."

"I think you'll figure it out—"

"Well, I would like to try."

I walk back over and stand in front of him. "Look, Nash. I like you—"

"And I like you. That's a good start."

"But my life's going to be law school for the next three years. I don't know how much time I'll have for a relationship."

He reaches out and takes my hand. The tingling starts again. "I've been thinking about that. You'll need some place quiet to study. Maybe you can come up to Blitzen Bay on the weekends and recharge—study, sleep. Whatever you want."

"I miss it up there. And it is the quietest place on earth."

"The quietest." He takes my backpack off my shoulder and puts it by his feet. He pulls me a little closer to him. "And if you're losing it during the week, I'll come down here and take you out to dinner or a movie or whatever. Give you a little break."

I take another step until I'm standing between his legs. He puts his arms around my waist and pulls me into him. I get the first whiff of his scent. I've been missing it so much since it faded from the flannel shirt I stole from him.

"So, did you just come down here because Kit asked you to?" I inhale deeply. He smells so good that I'm almost getting lightheaded.

"There's another reason," he says, taking his phone out of his pocket. "And it's way more important than Kit's mission."

He plays with the phone for a second and then hands it to me. I enlarge the picture he's pulled up.

"Oh my God! It's the chickens in the outfits!"

"Yeah, Mom sent me that picture," he says, laughing.

I look at it more closely. "The hats look like little berets. How'd your grandma get them to stay on their tiny heads?"

"I can't imagine they stayed there very long before they either fell off or one of the other chickens ate it off."

"Wait, is one of these chickens the hen that died?" I say, looking back down at the phone.

"I have no idea, but I'm so proud of the way you just used the words chickens and hen correctly."

"I've been practicing just in case I saw you again."

"You have, huh?" His hands slide down my body until they're resting on my butt. "I told Mom you had a problem with all the different chicken terms. She said she agreed with you."

"You told your mom about me?" I look up at him, tilting my head slightly.

"Yeah," he whispers.

"But, we've only kissed a couple of times—"

He brushes his lips against mine. As my arms crawl up his chest and wrap around his neck, he guides my head into his as his mouth covers mine. He pulls me to him. My hands start weaving through his messy curls. He pulls his mouth back from mine and starts giving me little kisses all over my face.

"There, I've kissed you three times now," he whispers. "Do you want to go for four?

Epilogue

NASH

January 20
Los Angeles, California

"Okay, obviously this is why you didn't want me to talk to you. All you needed to say was that you had a boyfriend."

I hear a male voice coming from behind Elle. I pull her in for one last kiss. We've been making out for about ten minutes—me, sitting on the wall with her pulled between my legs. I think we're on about our twentieth kiss, but I've lost count.

I look up to see a random guy staring at us. "You know him?"

Elle turns around and rests her back against my chest. I pull her closer as the guy takes a step toward us.

"I didn't want you to talk to me because you're a misogynistic asshole. It has nothing to do with him," she says, draping her arms over my legs.

The guy shakes his head. "I've never understood why women can't just take a compliment."

I kiss Elle on the top of the head and then look up at the guy. "I love compliments. Why don't you try one on me? Let's see where it takes us."

He starts shifting back and forth. "I think I'm going to pass—"

"Aww, man, that's too bad. I'm a little hurt you can't come up with anything nice to say about me."

He backs up a few steps.

"Hey, bud, don't talk to my girlfriend again," I say as he starts to turn away from us. "That's your first and only warning. You understand that?"

"Yeah, man," he mumbles as he walks away.

Elle spins back around to face me. She's smiling. "Wait, I've gone from your friend to your girlfriend in about ten minutes."

"Does that bother you?"

"Not at all," she whispers in my ear as she starts to nibble on it. "Maybe we can go back to my place and try some of those other things I want you to do to me."

I put my hands on her cheeks and kiss her gently one more time. "I have one condition."

"Wow, okay. I wasn't expecting conditions," she says, laughing. "Let's have it."

"If we're going to try this," I say, putting my forehead against hers, "you have to promise me when I say or do something stupid—and I'm going to—you have to talk to me about it and tell me you have a problem instead of running away."

She nods. "I promise. Just don't try to get me to quit law school."

"I would never do that," I say, pushing her back a little bit so I can look at her. "Whatever you want to do, I'm going to have your back. Just talk to me about stuff. And if you have a problem, tell me."

She nods. "I will. But you have to talk to me, too. You're not exactly open."

"If you want to know something, ask me, okay? I'll answer any question."

"That's dangerous," she whispers as she brushes her cheek against mine.

"No, it's not. I want to tell you stuff. You might get sick of listening to me."

"Never." She takes my hand. "You want to get out of here?"

"Yeah." I jump down from the wall. "Am I keeping you from class? I don't want you to get demerits or whatever."

"No, I'm done for the day."

"Are you hungry? I'll buy you lunch."

She holds up her hand. "I have a problem."

"Yeah, I will not be listening to that problem." I walk over to the trash can to throw my coffee cup away. When I turn around, she still has her hand up. "Put your hand down and keep it to yourself. You're a starving college student. I'm buying for the next three years. After that, when you become a rich lawyer, you're buying."

She lowers her hand and smiles. "You're going to be around for three years?"

"Only if you quit bugging me about paying for stuff."

I take her hand and start leading her toward my truck. She pulls back on it. I turn around to look at her again. Her long, wavy hair is blowing gently in the ocean breezes. Her eyes are sparkling in the sun. I feel like I'm finally seeing her in her natural habitat.

I smile at her and pull on her hand again, but she doesn't move. I take a step back toward her and see that her eyes are starting to water.

"What? Why are you crying? Is it the chickens again?"

She shakes her head slowly as the tears start to stream down her cheeks. "No, I'm just happy. Really happy."

I pull her closer to me and smile. "You cry when you're happy, too?"

"All the time," she says, burying her head in my chest. "I know you probably think that's weird."

"I don't think it's weird. I think it's perfect." I pull her to me.

"I'm going to need a minute."

"All right. You know that's what my chest is made for—cry as much as you want."

She takes a shaky breath. "It's going to be a lot, Nash."

"I know, babe," I say, kissing the top of her head. "And it's all going to be okay. I promise."

What's Next?

In the second book of The Blitzen Bay Series, *No One Wants That*, Kit heads back to Blitzen Bay for summer vacation and gets involved in a bit of a love triangle with Mateo and Butch from The Trident Trilogy and *Raine Out*.

No One Wants That will be published in May 2022. It's now available for pre-order on Amazon. Sign up for my email newsletter at donnaschwartze.com to be the first to know when it's published.

In the meantime, my other books will give you insight into some characters you will see in *No One Wants That*.
    - The Trident Trilogy (*Eight Years, The Only Reason, Wild Card*) introduces Raine, Butch, Mason, and Millie.
    - The Grand Slam Series (*Truth or Tequila* and *Raine Out*) introduces Alex and continues the stories of Raine and Butch.
    All of my books can be read as standalone novels, but you

What's Next?

might appreciate them more if you know the back stories of the other characters.

All of my books are available on Amazon.

The Trident Trilogy (Eight Years, The Only Reason, and Wild Card)

Eight Years

A Navy SEAL protector romantic suspense novel that can be read as a standalone or as part of The Trident Trilogy. A strong woman. An overly protective man. When their clashing wills put her quest in danger, will she sacrifice her love or her life?

Millie Marsh is obsessed with finding the truth. Still mourning her beloved father's passing, the fierce CIA agent has poured all her energy into solving the mystery of her real mother's identity. So when she's saddled with a designated protector on a dangerous mission that could finally give her the answers she's sought, the driven woman barely spares the handsome man a second glance.

Mason Davis doesn't do relationships. But the jaded Navy SEAL's latest assignment watching the back of a sweet, smart, and strong-willed operative has him ready to break his own rules. And undeterred by her apparent lack of interest, the relentless alpha male channels his strategic training into breaking down her defenses.

Focused on the payoff of her years-long quest, Millie

desperately tries to ignore her attraction to her companion's well-muscled frame and hidden tender heart. And Mason fears that as they zero in on a terrorist cell, the first woman to touch his soul will fall to enemy fire.

Will the duo's red-hot chemistry scar them for life, or will they surrender to a happy ending?

"High heat and nail-biting suspense!!!!! I was sucked into Millie and Mason's world within minutes! Brilliant storyline and such likable characters that you can't help but fall in love with! Mason is just the right amount of tough alpha hero and a soft squishy heart that just might have met his match in Millie! Outstanding read!" Amazon Review

"It's been a while since I found a book that I couldn't put down. Loved the storyline, the characters and the writing are very well done. I can't wait to finish the series. Definitely recommend!" Amazon Review

"This book deserves so much more then 5 stars. I literally couldn't stop turning the pages. I had to know all about Millie's life, how everything was going to turn out. I went right on to the second book. Such a nice escape." Goodreads Review

The Grand Slam Series (Truth or Tequila and Raine Out)

Truth or Tequila

What's Next?

A steamy romantic comedy. Seb's the most famous baseball player in the world. Sophie's not impressed. Game on.

Sophie

When we graduated from college, my friends and I made a pact that we would only play this stupid game five more times—at each of our bachelorette parties. Tonight's number four, and it couldn't come at a worse time. I have a meeting with a new client tomorrow and I can't be hungover. Unfortunately, I've never played this game without ending up that way. I'm already at a disadvantage with the client. It's the professional baseball team in town. I'm not much of a sports fan. I don't even know who the players are, but I guess I'll worry about that tomorrow. Tonight, it seems that, once again, I'm destined for tequila and bad decisions.

Seb

Don't get me wrong, I like being a professional baseball player. I just wish it didn't come with so much fame. People are always staring at me, and tonight's no exception. All eyes are on me as I walk into the bar—except for one pair. And they're attached to a gorgeous woman. When she finally looks up from her phone, she catches me ogling her and rolls her eyes. I don't think she has any idea who I am. Damn, that turns me on. I spend most of the night trying to figure out how to talk to her when suddenly she lands in my lap. Apparently, she's playing a drinking game with her friends and has to get me to kiss her to win. I want to kiss her—passionately—but not when she's this flat-out drunk. I'd at least like her to remember our first kiss.

The Next Day

Sophie

I'm painfully hungover. All I want to do is get done with this meeting, so I can go home and have my friends tell me about the guy I tried to drunkenly seduce last night. All I remember are his eyes—his beautiful, soft blue eyes. My new client has me down on the field watching the players practice. Suddenly, the catcher jumps up from behind the plate and starts walking aggressively toward me. When he pulls up his mask, the eyes I've been thinking about all morning are staring at me. "Sophie?" he says as a smile starts curling at the corners of his mouth.

"I absolutely LOVED the plot idea. It was fun. The characters were fun...Seb and Sophie are the CUTEST couple ever." Goodreads Review

"Truth or Tequila has to be one of my favorite books I've read this year. The storyline holds your attention and the characters have you flipping pages!!!" Goodreads Review

"This book was just what I needed. A fun rom com, laugh out loud story with a little bit of everything. Sports romance, suspense, and a sweet love story." Goodreads Review

Be Social With Me

Facebook: @donnaschwartzeauthor and Donna Schwartze Reader Group

Instagram: @donnaschwartzeauthor

TikTok: @donnaschwartzeauthor

Goodreads: @donnaschwartze

About the Author

Donna Schwartze is the bestselling author of The Trident Trilogy (*Eight Years*, *The Only Reason*, and *Wild Card*), The Grand Slam Series (*Truth or Tequila* and *Raine Out*), and *The Runaway Bride of Blitzen Bay*. She is a graduate of the University of Missouri School of Journalism. She also holds a Master of Arts from Webster University. Be the first to know when a new book publishes in your favorite series by signing up for her email list at donnaschwartze.com.

Made in United States
Orlando, FL
07 April 2022